D1327378

THE MILFORD SERIES

Popular Writers of Today

VOLUME EIGHT

The Space Odysseys of Arthur C. Clarke

George Edgar Slusser

R. REGINALD

THE **Borgo Press**

SAN BERNARDINO, CALIFORNIA

MCMLXXVIII

To Karen and Edouard
in memory of Herr Weiss

Library of Congress Cataloging in Publication Data:

Slusser, George Edgar.
    The space odysseys of Arthur C. Clarke.

    (The Milford Series) (Popular Writers of Today; v. 8)
    Bibliography: p.
    1. Clarke, Arthur Charles, 1917-   —Criticism and interpre-
tation. I. Title.
PR6005.L36Z88   823'.9'14   77-24438
ISBN 0-89370-212-9

Produced, designed, and published by R. Reginald, The Borgo Press,
P.O. Box 2845, San Bernardino, CA 92406. Composition by Mary A.
Burgess. Cover design by Judy Cloyd.

First Edition————July, 1978

THE ODYSSEY PATTERN:
PROGRESS AND CLARKE'S ELEGAIC HUMANISM

The basic problem Arthur C. Clarke poses to the critic of science fiction is method—what is the most fruitful way to approach his work? A recent, and on the whole excellent, collection of essays on Clarke (in the Writers of the Twenty-first Century Series) raises this problem by its very diversity of views. Individual weaknesses and disparities—both in literary form and in theme—are isolated. These visions remain partial, however. No comprehensive pattern is sought; there is no systematic attempt to define the working relationship between form and ideas in Clarke, or to explain this process by inserting it in some larger frame of reference—literary and cultural tradition. My debt to these pioneering essays is obvious. In this study, however, I attempt to go further. In pursuing what I call the "Odyssey pattern," I seek to define a central organizing structure in Clarke's fiction, one which bears interesting and precise analogies to the writer's cultural and social situation and hence to ours. If all literature possesses such significant structures, Clarke's work is of particular interest for its angle of vision—here is a scientist writing about the quandary of modern scientific man, drawing on deep and persistent currents of Western literature. This firm grounding in the "two cultures" alone would make Clarke worthy of our attention. As we shall discover, there is much more.

There are numerous ways to look at Clarke—the Twenty-First Century essays provide a representative sweep. The SF writer Algis Budrys (*Galaxy*, October 1967) had early accused Clarke of cultivating a commercially successful formula: he has built "a formidable reputation for profundity by repeating, over and over again, that the universe is wide and man is very small." David Samuelson's essay refines this idea: *Childhood's End* is a botched attempt to achieve literary "maturity" in an as-yet immature genre, dominated on one hand by bug-eyed monsters and pulp cliches, on the other by a vision of things irrationally hostile to science. "The whole however is flawed, not only by deficiencies in style, characterization, and narrative structure, which could presumably be corrected by revision, but also by a fundamental dichotomy between opposing goals." In his article on Clarke's "aliens," E. Michael Thron sees things in a totally different light: "We, as literary critics, might fuss about artistic completeness but shouldn't we, as members of a group of readers who want

3

speculation, be fussing about the idea and the future possibilities of that idea as a reality?'' Thron here is taking exception, not to Samuelson, but to John Huntington's argument in another of these essays: that Clarke's novels are marked by discontinuity between the mundane and the transcendent, by ''disjunction'' between technological progress and its suspension in mysticism.

However divergent, all these studies have two things in common: each perceives, on one level or another, a problematic or divided structure. And each, in the face of this, seeks to exonerate Clarke, to take the blame from him and lay it somewhere else. To Samuelson, it is the genre and not the writer that is ultimately at fault. For Huntington the cause is the ''dilemma of progress'' itself—on the contrary, Clarke has resolved this cultural rift with ''ingenuity.'' And for Thron the burden lies not with the writer but the reader: it is he who refuses to see this triumph of the alien, ''not as an esthetic solution, but as a prediction of the solution to our culture.'' What these maneuvers do—insistently—is raise the problem of the relation of the writer to some larger frame of reference. But none of the critics considers this relation systematically, or seeks to broaden the frame to include the widest variety of factors, collective and cultural as well as individual, unconscious as well as premeditated. Is it necessary, for instance, to choose (as Thron would have us do) between form and ''ideas?'' Instead of asking how well or badly Clarke uses such literary devices, we would do better to see how he employs the ones he does, and to what end. Nor are the ''relevance'' of his predictions or the ''ingenuity'' of his solutions *per se* as interesting as the ways in which these—more even than the dilemmas they purport to solve—might mirror relationships, and significant changes in relationships, between modern individual man and society, nature, or God. If we are to treat Clarke as a writer of ideas, let it be in a more sophisticated sense. More than characters or wise pronouncements in Clarke (the first are usually flat, the second commonplace), the reader notices the insistence with which he returns to the same ambiguous pattern over and over. Ambiguity is not some anomaly to be excused or circumvented. On the contrary, it is the central ''idea'' in Clarke: an idea that is inseparable from formal configurations, one not ''said'' but expressed in the structural dynamics of the work itself.

Only one essay in the above-mentioned collection makes a partial attempt to insert Clarke's fiction in a broader context of human activity—Betsy Harfst's study of "mythological content." Its limitations are equally instructive. Four novels (*Childhood's End*, *2001: A Space Odyssey*, *Rendezvous with Rama* and *Imperial Earth*) are seen to correspond (simultaneously) with the four stages of Jung's transformation myth, and the four planes of Eastern mythology. This "tetralogy" is supposedly a subtle work of syncretic thought, in which the opposing dynamics of East and West, intuition and reason, are blended. In it Clarke "theorizes that when mankind has learned to reconcile the two abilities a balanced, creative intellectual maturity will be achieved." Ideas are being sought in structures; nevertheless, the problems with this method are clear. First of all, why deal only with these four works, and none of the others?. Nor are the four in chronological order—*Childhood's End* is an early novel (1953), and *2001* is either a collective effort, or a patchwork of shorter, earlier tales, or both. The structure Harfst uncovers is incredible in its density and coherence—all ambiguities vanish in the many levels of mythical interpretation. All, perhaps, but the most fundamental ambiguity: for it is not clear whether Clarke consciously built this impressive structure, or whether myth is shaping itself. An example is the meaning of Bowman's name. Harfst tells us it derives "from the Anglo-Saxon *beow* meaning *barley*, a seed grain, or from the Old English *boga* meaning *bow* or *rainbow*." By stretching things, this knot of possibilities can be reduced to system—will and the flower of selfhood taken up in the mandala of this name. Yet even assuming that names are significant to Clarke, we wonder just how much of this figured in his choice here. Is not the fact that Frank Poole's first name is Kelvin in the earlier versions of *2001* just as revelatory of some "secret design"? Pursuing this track at least has the virtue of carrying us back from the most generalized mythical patterns to a specific period and problem: nineteenth century science, and the nature and limitations of scientific systems. In her rage for order and meaning, Harfst not only ignores the ambiguities of the structures she deals with, but, more importantly, obscures the relationship of these structures to the immediate cultural situation of the writer: scientific man at the crossroads of technological progress and spiritual anxiety.

Harfst mentions irony in passing. But she never considers that Clarke's use of "myth" or cultural allusion might partially (or primarily) be just that. The name Bowman, for instance, might simply be an ironic reference to the hero of that earlier

5

epic of voyage and return which serves as titular model here. In the epilogue to his *Lost Worlds of 2001*, Clarke makes this obvious parallel clear: 'When Odysseus returned to Ithaca, and identified himself in the banqueting hall by stringing the great bow that he alone could wield, he slew the parasitical suitors who for years had been wasting his estate.'' Will the Star Child returning to Earth follow Homer's transfigured hero? Here is another resonance ironically imparted to an already ambiguous ending, and a valuable insight into the pattern of this novel and Clarke's sense of structure in general. It is reasonable to assume that Clarke would be fascinated with *The Odyssey*, for the very essence of its form is ambiguity. Moreover, that form shapes and controls exactly the same oppositions that Huntington and Thron isolate in Clarke's work: the alien and the mundane, the domestic and the transcendent. In the travels of Odysseus (as with those of Bowman), beginning and end are at one and the same time coincident (Phaeacia and Ithaca are adjacent lands) and antipodal. The narrative line itself is built on two opposing and contradictory strands—progress and stasis. In the act of going out the hero is simultaneously coming back; his voyage is simultaneously an exploration of the fabulous and a homecoming. In the same manner, the miraculous and the commonplace exist together in *The Odyssey*. Just as the posts of the hero's fabled symbolic bed are living trees rooted in his native soil, so the transcendent grows out of the most banal everyday objects and actions: Odysseus's baths, Athena's golden lamp amid the domestic torches. In *2001* this pattern merely emerges to a new degree of self-consciousness.

A closer look, however, reveals that a similar dynamic informs the scientific odysseys of almost all Clarke's heroes. To claim that Clarke here is consciously rewriting *The Odyssey*—even with irony—is absurd, of course. The famous epic does, however, embody an archetypal situation. The archetype is qualified, though: "eternal" human rhythms are shaped by cultural patterns firmly rooted in Western tradition. Clarke is simply a modern heir to this tradition; in his work the older pattern has undergone significant changes in answer to the new pressures of his society. Less than a myth, but more than a simple trick or literary device, Clarke's "Odyssey pattern" is what Lucien Goldmann calls a "cultural fact." I propose to study it in terms of Goldmann's structural sociology—a method which seeks homological relationships between just such a fundamental literary structure and the mental structures or "world view" of the social group that produces an author and his works.

Goldmann's method has two complementary phases—to comprehend and to explicate. Simply to describe the pattern and its alterations or developments is not enough; these must also be "inserted" in the intellectual or social groups which give rise to them. For Goldmann, social group is primarily social class—his bias is that of Marxist economics. Certainly Clarke's ambiguities can be "explicated" profitably in this light: here is a representative of the scientific middle class, with roots in nineteenth-century capitalism. Torn asunder by the inherent contradictions of his class's world view, he is doomed to chronicle progress, and to deny it at the same time. Clarke's pattern, however, is both less and more than this—it touches other problematic aspects of Western cultural tradition as well. On one hand, it is curiously limited, parochial even, grounded in a literary and scientific heritage that is specifically English. American SF, grappling with the same critical relationship between individual scientific man and his world, produces a different basic pattern, one with opposite emphasis. On the other hand, it (like its American counterpart) is nonetheless the mirror of a general crisis in Western humanist tradition, to which Marxism is no more than another proposed solution with its own roots in a specific social group.

If in one area I stretch the parameters of Goldmann's method, in another—that of judging Clarke's value as a writer—I adhere to it strictly. This at least will bring to bear different criteria than the usual "convincing characters" or "unified plot"—the standards of the realist norm. To Goldmann "the great writer is precisely that exceptional individual who succeeds in creating in a given domain—that of the literary work—an imaginary universe which is rigorously coherent or almost so, the structure of which corresponds to that *toward which* the group he represents *is tending*." The group then is changing, evolving, the work more or less coherent—the relation of the two is one of dynamic interchange. The mediocre work is an abstraction—the static, dead reflection of a collective consciousness that is vital. Great writing, on the other hand, is alive to the point of actually being a "constitutive factor" in shaping this consciousness. If criticism sees in Clarke a modern "mystic" or speculator, it should do so in this perspective. What might seem to the traditional eye artistic weaknesses or faults can then be reinterpreted as possibly significant structual alterations in response to contradictions or limitations in the underlying world view.

The goal here is not to excuse bad writing, or suspend old values with some new form of casuisty, but to ask new questions: how flexible and complex is Clarke's pattern? Is he content merely to reflect the confusions of modern scientific man, thus simplifying or even falsifying them; or does he give to these a "rigorous coherence," handing man's dilemma back to him in a clearer form? These standards should do justice to Clarke as a writer of ideas while at the same time better defining the ways in which he is precisely that.

At the heart of most of Clarke's fiction is the problem of human progress. That problem may, however, run deeper than many critics have seen. Invariably, the process has two steps: utopia and transcendence—the end of man's evolution, and the beginning of some new, superhuman phase of development. But Clarke's view is not serenely macro-historical: he does not simply resolve the utopian dilemma—stagnation at the end—by giving mankind some greater cosmic destiny. On the contrary, his stories and novels reflect the anxieties of humanist science facing a future it is helping to bring about. The price man must pay for continued progress is the human form divine. Technology too bears the seeds of its own dissolution: man achieves rational control over his environment, only to relinquish it to some higher, inscrutable fatality. Clarke's response to this dilemma is interesting. Instead of opting for one or the other, man or progress, he chooses both. His characters invariably go out, and this invariably leads to suspension of the human: whether they are dwarfed by the alien, or themselves lifted to another, alien plane of existence, the result is the same. This going out is balanced by a coming back, progress by preservation. If man loses his humanity, he paradoxically reaffirms it at the same time. Levels are changed in the process. What stands in opposition both to utopia and transcendence is, in Northrop Frye's term, the "individual varieties of experience." In Clarke's world, clearly, the individual who abides is not the old action hero. On the contrary, he gradually loses his function, first in the utopian world of comfort and plenty, then finally and irrevocably in the mystical resignation of the end. But as "active" man is lost, a new man is retrieved—the hero has become lyrical observer. At the limits of human experience, Clarke's new voyager can no longer affirm man's essence by acts of defiance, but by lament. He discovers that among the alien there is no place for man in his present form. As he does so, however, he in turn "humanizes" the alien by infusing it with a lyrical sadness heightened by this sense of exclusion and loss. In reading Clarke, invariably one thinks of Pascal's reed. In Pascal's vision, man discovers he is a helpless nothing against the vastness of the universe: "But though the universe crushes him, man is more noble than it because he knows he is dying and knows the advantage the universe has over him. The universe knows nothing." For Clarke, however, what "makes" man in the face of blank indifference is no longer reason or knowledge, but something far more solitary and passive. In his stories and novels, the lyric beauty that briefly transforms these infinite silences is that of elegy.

The evocation of Pascal is significant, for already in the seventeenth century tension between scientific speculation and humanistic beliefs had become acute. It reached its extreme degree before the breaking point only in the nineteenth century. Clarke is considered by many to be a particularly "modern" speculator. It is thus interesting that, to seek analogies to Clarke's pattern and tone, one is invariably borne back to this earlier century of tension, to literary works and scientific theories of the *fin de siecle*. Clarke's response to the dilemma of human progress as modern science conceives it is oddly ambiguous. The split between man and such inexorable, inhuman processes as evolution appears to be more radically accepted in our century. An example is the bitter prediction of Sir Charles Darwin (a grandson of the great Darwin) in his book *The Next Million Years* (1952) that man can progress no farther: "to do better will require a brand new species." Clarke faces this prospect neither with the cosmic rapture of a Stapledon nor with a retreat to faith in man's eternity. Instead he embraces both man and his passing. His tone is rather the elegaic weariness of Wells's Time Traveller, who contemplates an end-of-the-world landscape barren of man, only to return to the mediocrities of his Edwardian drawing room. Another close parallel is seen in J. H. Rosny's equivocal novel *The Death of the Earth* (1912). On one level, this is a tale of evolution. The earth of the future is a desiccated hulk, where mankind has been superceded by a kingdom of enigmatic mineral life-forms. On another, however, it is one long protracted lament of an expiring humanity. As the title suggests, the death of man is the death of the Earth: in spite of objective, "scientific" vision, his is the only form of life that counts. In Clarke, as in both these works, an individual lyrical voice is raised against inexorable, inhuman forces.

To evolution, in fact, Clarke seems to prefer entropy. Perhaps in this light, Astronaut Poole's lost first name is significant after all. Cecil Schneer, in his book *The Search for Order*, has this to say of Kelvin: "It was the death of Kelvin in 1907 and not the shot at Sarajevo in 1914 that brought an end to the comfortable world of the nineteenth century." Clarke also seems unwilling to take this leap into modernity. It is as if, faced with the vision of discontinuity, he turns back to the closed continuity of the thermodynamic system. Indeed, the analogies between his "Odyssey pattern" and this physical system are striking. In the latter, energy is both conserved and rendered unavailable. The "heat-death" of entropy, with all bodies resting in ultimate conformity of temperature, is an act of conservation as well: progress and stasis are linked in a continuous, systematic relationship. Clarke almost seems to transpose this system into moral and metaphysical realms. In this sense, his vision is less utopian or apocalyptic than it is entropic. Everywhere in his fiction, man's world is literally running down—his "utopias" such as Diaspar or New Atlantis are in the final stages of heat-death. Collective man no longer struggles or resists. Pushed by "progress" or pulled by some alien overseer, he moves inexorably toward a point of stasis. But if this appears (as it most clearly does in *Childhood's End*) a moment of transcendence—thus of further progress—it is actually a moment of conservation of human energy as well, in a form different but abiding. As man ceases to act, his powers to observe and intuit are augmented and he rediscovers wonder in the drab existence of everyday life. Set against progress and evolutionary patterns is this closed system of human energy. Both pessimism and optimism are suspended here by what can only be called an alchemical humanism. As energy becomes unavailable in the heroic sphere, it is gradually transmuted into the gold of lyricism.

This lyrical voice reborn in Clarke is also a product of the nineteenth century. In the isolated singer of the Romantic we have what is perhaps the ultimate expression of individualism in Western literary tradition. Already in the Romantic poets there was radical rupture between the subjective "poetic" individual and the objective natural processes modern science was describing and formulating into laws. Thus the famous attack on Newton's rainbow in Keats's "Lamia": "There was an awful rainbow once in heaven:/we know her woof, her texture; she is given/in the dull catalogue of common things." The battle lines here are drawn a certain way—opposing the scientist's vision of nature is not a collective or social idea of man but the radically isolated lyrical individual. Behind this rift between science and poetry are two modes of perceiving reality that become increasingly divergent and irreconcilable across the nineteenth century. If the indignation of the Romantic poets gradually gives way to elegaic resignation, it is because the mysteries of Earth are soon conquered by stronger things than "rule or line." The poet in 1890 must face the specter of evolution.

At this turn of the century, the true heir to the Romantics and their struggles with the method of science is Wells in his scientific romances. In Wells, emphases have drastically shifted. More significant here than differences, however, is the resiliency of a certain wider-lying pattern. *The Time Machine*, no more or less than Keats's "Ode to a Nightingale," qualifies as a modern version of *The Odyssey*: in both there is a voyage out and back, movement between poles of the wondrous and the commonplace. How Wells adapts this pattern is crucial, for Clarke will hardly go further—in a fundamental sense, "speculation" in Clarke can be said to stop with Wells's time travelling Odysseus. At first glance the Romantic voyage of the imagination seems to be reversed in *The Time Machine*. Instead of escaping from reason and technology through intuition or on "wings of song," the poet's mode of transportation is now the machine itself. To Keats's narrator, the voyage out is one of union with another—"already with thee"; he is called back from his visionary flight to isolation, the "sole self." In Wells, things seem exactly the opposite. Now, at the far end of his journey, it is a lonely Last Man who contemplates a dying Earth; when he returns, it is ironically to the most comfortable of societies—an English dinner party. But from Keats to Wells, are things really reversed? Closer to the truth is this: something present in Keats only as a tendency is firmly developed in Wells's romance. Keats's narrator goes to "faery lands," but they are "forlorn." And he returns both to the isolated self and to "familiar meadows." What Wells achieves is a violent rupture between his two polar domains of experience: the marvelous is made futile, no longer the realm of poetic inspiration but of elegy; and in making his everyday world not just familiar but banal—a smug, complacent British society—he renders it equally futile as well. In their self-sufficiency these two worlds seem hermetically sealed from each other. They appear to have no ties, and yet they do. There are two contending relationships, in fact—and here we are at the heart of Wellsian ambiguity. There is evolution and entropy. Indeed, we cannot escape this relationship by seeing the vision of the

11

end as a dream. The scientific "accuracy" of the description, the time machine itself, lends it authority or "reality"—this inhuman law is inexorable. And then there is the time traveler. Here (as in Keats) is a poet, a force eminently human, who joins disparate realms. The link of progress is an ironically gruesome one ("I grieved to think how brief the dream of the human intellect had been"). Yet this going forward is balanced by the traveler's return. Dreams dispelled are replaced by a momentary transfiguration of the everyday world—a dull catalogue of things once again becomes a source of wonder.

A curious scene in *The Time Machine* epitomizes this very Odyssean interpenetration of worlds and directions. On his way back home from the distant future, the Time Traveler again crosses the path of his housekeeper, Mrs. Watchett: "I think I have told you that when I set out. . . Mrs. Watchett had walked across the room, travelling. . . like a rocket. As I returned, I passed again across that minute when she traversed the laboratory. But now her every motion appeared to be the exact inversion of her previous ones. The door at the lower end opened, and she glided quietly up the laboratory, back foremost, and disappeared behind the door by which she had previously entered." The vast sweep of time suddenly contracts to a point, the marvelous grounds itself in the banal, the elegiac in the comical. But if familiar human space becomes the frame for these fabulous comings and goings, it in turn is made a wonder. Mrs. Watchett moving backward is an impossibility without the time machine, and the exceptional angle on the commonplace it provides. Upon his return, the narrator of Keats's "Nightingale" experiences his old world in terms of the new one he has just visited: "Do I wake or sleep?" The Time Traveler has a similar moment: "Around me was my old workshop again, exactly as it had been. I might have slept there, and the whole thing have been a dream. And yet, not exactly! The thing had started from the south-east corner of the laboratory. It had come to rest again in the north-west, against the wall where you saw it. That gives you the exact distance from my little lawn to the pedestal of the White Sphinx, into which the Morlocks had carried my machine." At one and the same time he is able to measure his "dream" in terms of this familiar space and prove it real, and to see this same solid domesticity infused with a new sense of its terrible end. In this process the ordinary is quickened, and the human observer raised to a new level of consciousness. The Time Traveler cannot stay, he must go out again. As with Mrs. Watchett, however, his own existence has become a simultaneous coming and going. If this lyrical hero evolves in his confrontation with the scientist's view of things, it is in a certain way. In traversing the space from the Romantics to Wells and Clarke, he may even become a scientist himself. But he always keeps a strong touch of the poet. This doubleness is significant. For what emerges from this line of development is less a row of forward-looking faces—man's voice everfading in the wake of an increasingly indifferent universe—than the Janus face, looking forward and backward simultaneously.

Clarke's work is a perfect example of this. Invariably, there is an adventure of human "progress." In some way or other a man journeys to contact with the unknown, and comes face to face simultaneously with the possibility of transcendence and the limits of his humanity. Invariably too, the going out is balanced by some sort of coming back. In these "homecomings" the voyager's wonder and resignation before the mysteries of the universe are recaptured (if only momentarily) in a trivial incident, infused into the most mundane object. "Out there," man is absorbed in human vastness; "in here," he reawakens new meaning in the everyday world, "humanizing" some microcosmic part of that greater nature. This is not linear advancement but oscillation, a form of perpetual motion. As with Wells's Time Traveler, homecoming leads to a new voyage: progress/stasis/progress. Out of these interpenetrating opposites a new set of Odyssean transformations arises. The final passage from *The Time Machine* shows how clearly Wells set this pattern. Like the Ancient Mariner, the Traveler returns to unsettle the narrator—this complacent bourgeois turns to morose speculation on man's destiny: "He, I know. . . thought but cheerlessly of the Advancement of Mankind, and saw in the growing pile of civilization only a foolish heaping that must inevitably fall back upon and destroy its makers in the end. If that is so, it remains for us to live as though it were not so. But to me the future is still black and blank. . . And I have by me, for my comfort, two strange white flowers—shrivelled now, and brown and flat and brittle—to witness that even when mind and strength had gone, gratitude and a mutual tenderness still lived on in the heart of man." Again, are we moving forward or standing still? The Traveler is gone, but his convert remains. And in these "strange white flowers," the commonplace and the wondrous meet, are held in balance. Yet it seems the flowers also have re-entered the destructive stream of time, for they wilt and fade. The 13 narrator is bounded by this same finite world; but it is his imagination this time which takes us on a fabulous voyage. Again, entropy carries us to the brink—the heroic virtues have run down and are no more. Yet these ruins are shorn up by heightened poetic intuition—new insight into the gentler human qualities of "gratitude" and "tenderness." The poetry that ennobles these flowers is that of dying mankind. *In extremis*, the only balance struck is that of the elegiac voice brooding on shrivelled remains. Even in his farthest vision, Clarke will go no farther in the exercise of this elegiac humanism.

Over his long career Clarke has written short fiction, novellas, and novels of different lengths. Cutting across such genre distinctions, Peter Brigg (in another article from the *Writers of the Twenty-First Century* collection) divides Clarke's output into "three styles": the hard extrapolater, the wit, and the mystic. Whatever diversity there is in Clarke, however, exists only on the surface. Indeed, anyone who reads great doses of his writing is struck by just the opposite—in spite of variations in tone or length, it is all very similar. This is due mainly to the underlying persistence of the Odyssey pattern. If themes and narrative situations vary, they hardly evolve. Instead, this basic matrix reduces them invariably to the same set of relationships. Moreover, instead of different or successive "sytles," the various tones of Clarke's writing are better described as different modes of a same and unique verbal figure—the oxymoron, a surprising and transformatory juxtaposition of opposites. If we wish to classify Clarke's work, we should do so rather in increments—to what degree is this single pattern developed in any given work? His range extends from various kinds of partial Odysseys to the most elaborate voyages and returns. Quite naturally (if not exclusively), these latter occur in the longer works. Clarke's general development as a writer, certainly, has been toward ever larger structures—his latest novel, *Imperial Earth*, is also his longest to date. For reasons of space and balance, the present study deals mainly with novels. This does not mean, however, that only Clarke's novels possess the intricacy of construction of a "full" Odyssey. On the contrary, Clarke continues to work in short forms; if anything, the development of his stories parallels that of his novels. In fact, a brief look at a few sample tales, taken in chronological order, provides an excellent view, in miniature, of Clarke's overall literary evolution. Not only do the stories tend to get longer, but the Odysseys they recount become more complex. We pass from simple juxtapositions of the "trick" or surprise ending to calm, extended workings-out of multi-layered sets of "correspondences"—the author's word for the intricate combinations of opposites he erects in *Imperial Earth.* Throughout all of this Clarke is doing little more than refining and perfecting techniques of variation on his single theme.

Ostensibly, "The Nine Billion Names of God" (1952) is a story of apocalypse. In reality, though, the process described here (in a manner wryly ironic, if not facetious) is an entropic one. A sect of Tibetan monks believe that the world will end when the nine billion names of God have been listed: "The human race will have finished what it was created to do, and there won't be any point in carrying on." In order to accelerate this task of naming names, the monks employ a computer—mystery is literally conquered by rule and line, the individuality and variety that abide in names are leveled and spent. And at the point of highest entropy—when no more names are available—a heat-death occurs: the stars go out. Simultaneous with this process, there is a curious reversal at work—one which builds and magnifies the individual vision in the face of an indifferent universe. The laconic description of the end ("there won't be any point in carrying on") is at the antipodes of poetic wonder. It is spoken by one of two computer programmers—men whose sole yearning is not for God or transcendence, but for home, family, and the familiar comforts. They are, in fact, on the road home when the end really does come. At this moment, suddenly, inexplicably, their banal vision is transfigured: mountains gleam "like whitely hooded ghosts," Chuck's face in the moonlight is "a white oval turned toward the sky." In an ironic switch, as if their former banality had been transferred to the awesome spectacle itself, revelation becomes something commonplace, almost domesticated: the stars go out "without a fuss." If mankind is superceded here, at the last minute the balance is tipped slyly in his favor. The luster of apocalypse is drained away as ordinary men and their homing instincts are uplifted in poetic wonder. In a brief flash before the darkness, the going out and coming home crisscross, becoming one. This is clever sleight of hand, but significant in terms of the Odyssey pattern.

The focus of a more famous tale, "The Star" (1954), is less the cosmic irony of its surprise ending—our star of Bethlehem was in reality a supernova that destroyed a paradisical world at the other end of the universe—then the voyage of its narrator, a Jesuit priest-scientist, to this destroyed world and back. It too seems essentially a journey to loss of faith, to man's encounter with his limits. But again, simultaneous with the going out is a coming back. Paradoxically, the hero's perception of cosmic indifference coincides with clear proof of the Christian religion—the Biblical account was correct after all, there was a Star of Bethlehem. In the same way, if one homeland must in the process be abandoned—the unbroken line from Christianity to humanist science is shattered by the irony of this discovery—it is only so that another may be found. It is here, at the farthest point of his journey, that this priest comes nearest to basic humanity: he observes the simple joys and everyday domestic pursuits of this "disturbingly human" race, and grieves. The final juxtaposition is that of a lyrically heightened voice brooding on the spectacle of universal indifference. Once more, at this extreme crossroads, a man reaches the ultimate expression of his individual humanity, only to have it become a lament. Religious belief and scientific method both give way to the elegaic question: "Yet, oh God, there are so many stars you could have used. What was the need to give these people to the fire, that the symbol of their passing might shine above Bethlehem?"

"Summertime on Icarus" (1960) takes a traditional enough theme—a crash and rescue on the asteroid Icarus—and handles it in a very particular way. This time the narrative focus is not on the hero's struggle to survive. He is physically trapped, helpless, resigned. What Clarke gives us is the vision of another man suspended at the crossroads, whose lyrical awareness of human insignificance is awakened and keyed to the pitch of a scream—the moment at which dissolution and homecoming again overlap. More clearly than before, perceptions of the inhuman machinery of the cosmos are linked in the hero's mind with analogies to familiar human things or situations—in this case a common myth: "How strange that he should be dying now, because back in the nineteen-forties—years before he was born—a man at Palomar had spotted a light on a photographic plate, and had named it so appropriately after the boy who flew too near the sun." The pull of the unknown is balanced by the known—here already is an example of those "correspondences" that Clarke will develop so elaborately in his later works. In the same manner, the hero's moment of transcendental vision leads simultaneously away from Earth and man, and back to it: "At some remote time in the past [Icarus] had been under enormous pressure—and that could mean only one thing. Billions of years ago it had been part of a much larger body, perhaps a planet like Earth. For some reason that planet had blown up. . .Even at this moment, as the incandescent line of sunlight came closer, this was a thought that stirred in his mind. What Sherrard was lying upon was the core of a world—perhaps a world that had known life. In a strange irrational way it comforted him to know that his might not be the only ghost to haunt Icarus until the end of time.''

The experiences of space adventurer Colin Sherrard are typical of many other Clarke heroes. His is a world in which heroism itself has been strangely domesticated. As part of the *Prometheus*'s crew he is the fire-stealer plucking ''unimagined secrets from the heavens''; but he is also a member of a routine research mission in connection with a very mundane ''International Astrophysical Decade.'' Even more strikingly, his ordeal itself is the exact opposite of action-adventure. Instead, an oddly entropic process, a series of ''moments of physical weakness,'' reduces him to a state of near-immobility. First an attack of ''space vertigo'' causes him to lose all purpose and direction, grounding him in disorder. Then the crippling of his ''space pod'' brings total rupture between volition and physical movement. Paradoxically, however, it is only at this point of stasis that Sherrard makes the discoveries these men have travelled millions of miles to get. Only when he experiences the sudden blast of the sun's heat in this helpless state does he understand what made Icarus a ''blasted cinder''—in measuring cosmic processes, instruments cannot replace a man. At this apparently fatal moment of truth there is another reversal. What comes to Sherrard is less a vision of man's annihilation, his nothingness in the face of indifferent vastness, than a heightened feeling for some abiding human presence at the center of things. Out of impending personal disaster surges a new vision of life (something like Heinlein's mystical ''fifth planet''), which in turn is caught up in still wider vistas of destruction. Set against this spiraling vortex of change is a counterfigure—suspension as in a mirror. The hero's death is overlayed by that of an entire race. And on this hypothetically Earth-like planet the ''ghosts'' he conjures up could be human ones. Once again a man plunges to the heart of the alien only to discover (and reaffirm) the familiar and the human. But again, as with the narrator of ''The Star,'' it is a humanity most fully sensed or understood only at the moment of its passing.

Sherrard doesn't actually die. In another twist he is retrieved and eventually returns home, a home which no longer seems the same. Here, in reverse fashion, the return to the familiar infuses it with an alien, transcendental quality. Near death, at the farthest point of alienation, Sherrard's return had already begun. Seeking to kill himelf by letting his oxygen escape, he is thwarted when the valve sticks, and literally forced into the lyrical alternative—a last glimpse of Earth brings a lament for lost loved ones and home. Cutting across this vision is a radically transcendent one: *"What was that?"* A brilliant flash of light, infinitely brighter than any of the stars, had suddenly exploded overhead. Miles above him a huge mirror was sailing across the sky. . . . Such a thing was utterly impossible." But this epiphanic mirror, in yet another reversal, seems to reflect back commonplace things. Sherrard's lament rises to a scream, only to sink back immediately into the ordinary world. To the listening captain who saves him, Sherrard's metaphysical despair is but a "shout": "Hold on, man! We've got a fix on you. But keep shouting!" In the same way his great "mirror" turns out to be no more (and no less) than one of his familiar radiation screens come now to protect a man instead of technical instruments from the sun's rays. We are not left here in domestic comfort, with every mystery explained away. When this Ulysses finally looks homeward again it is with a gaze contaminated by strangeness: "Back to enjoy and cherish all the beauties of the world he had thought was lost forever— No, not all of them. He would never enjoy summer again."

The elegaic poignancy and finality of "The Star" echoes that of its contemporary, *Childhood's End*, a novel which for all its promise of transcendence culminates in radical division: lamenting man is suspended in the face of cosmic process. "Summertime," on the other hand, in its brush with annihilation and mystical revelation, and its continuous rhythm of reversals that pours the marvelous into the familiar and back again, looks forward to the more sequential structure of a work like *2001*. A longer and more recent tale, "A Meeting with Medusa," is the harbinger of Clarke's latest novels, in which still another twist is given to the Odyssey pattern. Here in miniature are the reductive intricacies that shape *Imperial Earth*.

As an odyssey, as a voyage to fabulous places and back, "Medusa" resembles "Summertime"—an episode in an ongoing adventure rather than a totality. Similarly this story also makes constant use of suspending juxtapositions. But where these were employed before to strike a perilous balance between man and cosmos—to oppose the physical fact of change with the lyrical dream of permanence—now they have been turned to new, ironic ends. In "Medusa" even transcendence has become problematical. Before there was no doubt—evolutionary process would surpass man, the human form was not divine but transitional. There was no doubt either that man's lamenting dream, however futile, was also noble. Though man (at these moments of transcendental vision) sees he must pass, the fact that he can raise his voice against the blind mechanisms of evolution, and utter his desire to be the unchanging center of things, makes him (in a twist on Pascal's thinking reed) as great as the forces that crush him, for they know nor sing not. In this recent tale, however, these extremes are not simply suspended face-to-face—they are rather played against each other in mutually reductive fashion. Transcendence becomes less clearly progressive, a "childhood's end" or even the fleeting revelation of cosmic process. And the isolated lyrical hero on the edge is more an aberration than ever. Clearly in "Medusa" (as in his latest novels) Clarke is tending toward a new view of man; he has retreated from confrontation at the end of human mind or time to the restatement of a mean. In relation to his earlier elegaic humanism, Clarke seems not to have moved forward so much as backward, to have abandoned *fin de siecle* romanticism for satire, the voyage of the entropic discoverer for something closer to the travels of Gulliver. Howard Falcon's journey to greater-than-human powers and his moments of transcendence are ironically offset in such a manner that, as he becomes something more than man, he is simultaneously becoming less. What is displayed here is neither man's evolutionary potential nor his lyrical uniqueness, but rather his essentially normative nature.

The key to this process of reduction in "Medusa" is two sets of bracketing events. In this tale there is a symmetry and direction that (though composed of old elements and processes) seem new to Clarke. Previously his narratives were characterized by telescoping—in single events the voyage out and back, the alien and familiar, were made to meet and blend. In this story too, Earth and Jupiter—home and the field of Odyssean adventures—seem merely inversions of each other. A series of interpenetrating correspondences link these opposites and draw them together. They are pushed apart again, however—in polar suspension—by these bracketing sets of recurring situations: an event on Earth happens again on Jupiter, a meeting at the beginning is repeated at the end. We are now invited to seek differences in what seem similar happenings, to compare and contrast. Between these polarities arises a system of compensations and ironic adjustments that, resonating this time across the whole expanse of the story, undermine and cancel what otherwise appears to be the unbroken moral and physical advancement of the hero. The first polar set is the sudden drop of a lighter-than-air ship, on Earth and on Jupiter. The second is Falcon's meeting with the "superchimp" in his plummeting ship, mirrored in the end by his encounter with Webster and his own rise to "superman" As these horizontal correspondences play off against each other, man finds himself ironically framed in tight limits.

At first glance Earth and Jupiter strike us as mirror images of each other: the *Queen Elizabeth* gives way to the *Kon-Tiki*, another dirigible ("Hot-hydrogen" has replaced helium) sailing the "aerial sea" of the Jovian atmosphere and discovering a "medusa." If these two situations are vastly different (this new world "could hold a hundred Pacifics") yet they are strangely analagous, for the purpose of "sailing" here is also to defy the pull of the deep, Jovian gravity: "At the level where *Kon-Tiki* was drifting now. . . the pressure was five atmospheres. Sixty-five miles farther down it would be as warm as equatorial Earth, and the pressure about the same as the bottom of one of the shallower seas." Even this small sample serves to show just how slippery these apparently neat inversions are—the "air" of Jupiter combines elements of both land and sea. This incessant rhythm of polar comparisons, cutting back and forth between worlds, provides ironic insight in both directions. We see not only the strangeness of Jupiter constantly eluding man's arrogant attempts to measure and tame it, but at the same time his familiar world becoming more uncertain, less stable. The *Queen Elizabeth* for instance, seems to be more out of its element on Earth than its counterpart in deep space. If this new *Queen* now sails the airs instead of the seas, it is in answer to the whims of a bored post-industrial humanity seeking its pleasures in increasingly unnatural fashion. Indeed, if what seems right on Earth is actually wrong, on Jupiter the wrong turns out to be right after all—the *Kon-Tiki* functions, it does the job. Here too on another level is a twist, for this physical success only points to moral and metaphysical failing. The *Queen* was and is a luxury liner, but the *Kon-Tiki* implies radical adventure, exploration of the unknown. Falcon plunges to the heart of this strange world only to find a "medusa"—the wall he beats against is man's psychological need to domesticate the alien. On the other hand, it is on Earth, at the very center of the familiar, that Falcon actually has what is perhaps his most intense brush with the uncanny. All at once, inside the air sack of his *Queen*, he comes upon a startling new world, an inverted land with a "curiously submarine quality." In a flash air and sea merge, the huge trans-lucent gasbags of the ship become "mindless, harmelss jelly-fish." Falcon here is but a frail man before his fall. And yet his vision is not a fearful but a peaceful one. Ironically, the vision of the almost more-than-human hero in the atmosphere of Jupiter (where again air and sea are seen as one) is just the opposite: in panic he flees the advances of this alien "jellyfish."

At either end of this vast crisscrossing web of correspon-dences are the two answering situations—the twin fall of ships. Not only are these individual events ambiguous in themselves, but each throws ironic light on the other; in their mirror re-flections Falcon's progress is suspended. In the crash of the *Queen* a near-fatal fall actually turns out to be a moment of transcendence: the decorative captain of a pleasure ship rises from the flames an insatiable Odysseus: decadent man is "reborn" a superman. At the end of his Jovian adventure Falcon openly asserts this new being, prides himself on his role as "ambassador between old and new." But this is exactly what he fails to be in his second fall over Jupiter. For instead of implementing the "prime directive" and making this first con-tact between man and alien life form, he panics and lets his ship drop away from the hovering Medusa. Once again he seems to fall only to rise higher. This time in fact he appears to pass beyond human honors and deeds alike: "He said 'men'. He's never done that before. And, when did I hear him use the word 'we'? He's changing, slipping away from us." But he has fallen too. This time the plunge is a moral rather than a physical one—he who would become more than man has through fear perhaps become less. In almost Swiftian fashion, through all these reversals, these falls and swellings of pride, runs a median, the human norm as measure of all things. Falcon's initial reaction to Jupiter confirms this standard: "He did not feel that Jupiter was huge, but that *he* had shrunk—to a tenth of his normal size. Perhaps, with time, he would grow accustomed to the inhuman scale of this world; yet as he stared at the unbelieveably distant horizon, he felt as if a wind colder than the atmosphere around him was blowing through his soul." Here is another "fall," one which serves to reduce the cosmic to manageable human dimensions. At once, however, things expand, and a touch of the old elegaic wonder returns as man again must confront infinite spaces. At this point we seem closer to the rhythmic relationship of man and God's universe in Pascal than in Swift: "If he exalt himself, I humble him; if he humble himself, I exalt him." Yet, as Falcon's tale unfolds, we soon see that this dynamic is parodied, itself treated reductively. In a final burst of pride Falcon rises "on his hydraulics to his full seven feet of height." By his act he proves that to "grow accustomed" to inhuman vistas is to be human no more. Again with irony all the more savage for its understatement balance is achieved: these extra inches were given to him to "compensate for what he lost in the crash of the *Queen*. However grotesquely, the human median holds.

In more way than one Falcon exalts himself only to be humbled. This rhythm of oscillation around a median functions here in a horizontal sense as well, and tends to offset the process of evolution itself. At first glance the twin "superchimp"—superman encounters may appear to mark successive stages in the hero's development. As man looks on ape, so superman looks on man: Falcon's past, present, and future seem spread before us. But if we look closer, we see that the two episodes are actually ironic inversions of each other: in the end Falcon rises and man descends, but in the beginning it is Falcon who descends and the chimp who rises. The hero himself links these two scenes: at the moment he takes leave of his old friend Webster, he suddenly recalls the instant inside the sinking *Queen* when he had faced the terrified "superchimp" on the ladder. It is he, in fact, who discovers their deeper affinity. In his mind, it is not Webster but himself who replaces the chimp in the equation. Linear evolution is suspended as two extremes—both deviants from the human norm—suddenly face each other: "Neither man nor beast, it was between two worlds, and so was he." This juxtaposition casts ironic light on Falcon's subsequent assertion of "somber pride in his uniqueness." Because he can go where man cannot, he feels he has advanced beyond him. But the "superchimp" was also an advancement over his species, a creature that in the terror of the crash "atavistically" reverted to its original nature as an ape. In like manner, Falcon, far from proving in his Jovian odyssey that he is more than human, becomes man again through his fear of the Medusa.

The various species in "Medusa" seem to exist not in genetic relationship to each other, but as isolated compartments, essentially disconnected states of being. What is "super" in both chimp and man is merely an accretion, the work of medical engineering. Each of these figures, in becoming greater than his species, simultaneously becomes less; each is a hybrid, a monstrous deviant from its respective norm. Things will change and go forward, but man as man will not: "Someday the real masters of space would be machines, not men, and he was neither." Falcon sees himself as the "first immortal midway between two orders of creation." Actually he is in the same extreme position as Clarke's earlier elegaic heroes. As with the lone wanderer of Matthew Arnold's "Stanzas from the Grande Chartreuse," he too is "between two worlds, one dead/The other powerless to be born." Falcon's hubris blinds him to this truth: at this point pride in his "uniqueness" is grotesque mock-heroics; visionary lament is replaced by Byronic posturing. In a tale where elegy has shaded into satire, what abides in the face of cosmic indifference is a human norm, the common term between beast-man and man-machine.

Clarke's reenactment of this pattern of contradictions and paradoxes in work after work seems almost a ritualistic act. Again and again his hero is painstakingly placed in his social setting, only to be yanked from it—the adventure is invariably a solitary one. More surprisingly, it is passive as well—the hero is less actor than a spectator to the drama of evolution. Clarke flaunts both evolution and relativity, for however much the protagonist may "move" in time, or see the most fearful changes, he remains firmly anchored in space. It is important that Wells's time machine has the form of a chair—the domesic object that most signifies stasis has itself become the source of movement. The machine has real affinities with the dinner guests' armchairs that surround it. Its center of gravity, however, goes beyond the merely contemporary and comfortable to much more permanent, unyielding foundations. If the Morlocks and Eloi have clearly evolved beyond man as we know him, the Traveller nevertheless seeks to draw them back into a human space that is less the familiar than the ideal: "[they have] kept too much of the human form not to claim my sympathy." Even when staring upon the unhuman landscape at the end, he can still affirm this form, if only in its absence. At once the space he occupies is a familiar one again: "Now in this old familiar room it is more like the sorrow of a dream than an actual loss." Clarke's adventurers are also often seated and immobile; and there is little actual loss or change, either. To contact the unknown is to return immediately to known space—the pilot seat becomes a chair again. And there are deeper roots: beneath the comfortable present lies an elegaic one—the perennial sorrow of the dream of human permanence. To Thoreau such a lament for the golden age was little more than a lament for golden men. And so it is for Clarke.

Here perhaps is the most striking paradox in his works: the writer who poses as poet of evolution, chronicler of the relativity of intelligences and life-forms, in reality uses his sweeping adventures to reaffirm a view of man which, in its almost idyllic insistence on family and hearth as the center of society, the focus of human endeavor, is profoundly aristocratic in nature. In all the comings and goings of Clarke's fictional universes, the values that define human space remain more than conventional and hieratical—Odysseus's royal bed becomes Wells's time-machine throne.

Such paradoxes, of course, are the stuff the Goldmann-inspired critics feed upon, for they seem to mirror deeper patterns of struggle within the writer's own class and society. The French critic Gerard Klein (himself a science fiction author and professional economist) has sought, for instance, to explain a related phenomenon—the rise of apocalyptic pessimism in American SF of the 60s, a period of unprecedented economic and technological growth—by seeing in this inconsistency the mark of the writers' own "disenfranchisement," the avowal that the intellectual class to which they belong no longer exercises control over the auto-regulated economy, the dehumanizing processes of modern capitalist society. The only place they still wield power is in their novels: there, over and over again, they damn to flames and destruction the system that excludes them (*Science Fiction Studies* 4:1, 3-13). It is possible to see in Clarke's Odyssey pattern a similar avowal: this time it is the bourgeois scientist who finds himself powerless to bring about his new world, to establish his technocracy on Earth, just as Wells's vision of the Cabals in *Things to Come* did nothing to forestall the blind machinery of World War II. Clarke's works, then, become tales of impotence and guilt in which the writer/scientist, through his narrative rhythms, seeks to reassert control over processes (physical and social) which he has discovered or formulated but been unable to direct, and which are now slipping entirely from his grasp. Once again the writer damns. Invariably, Clarke confronts short-term technological optimism with long-term evolutionary pessimism. Not only is human progress denied, but the efforts of man to advance are cruelly mocked in story after story: the moment chosen for revelation of man's cosmic insignificance is constantly his farthest point of technical success—a pioneering moon or space exploration. Behind such reductive processes we find the author playing god in his own creation, taking man to the brink of nothingness, only to snatch him back at the last moment unharmed. And yet, though he wields this double power of destructive scientific vision and redeeming mysticism, this author's dynamic proves sterile and self-cancelling in the end. What remains is only a helpless litany for worlds and values that are gone. In the adventures of Clarke's entropic Odysseus, we find that same "absence of social project" which Klein sees in American SF. In this light, Clarke does not look forward to classless utopias or progress for the masses but backward to that contradiction in terms, the bourgeois aristocrat, the "exceptional" man of Romantic lore, the alienated artist as solitary nightingale. Clarke's golden dream is thus doubly displaced.

Such an interpretation is tempting, for it digs at structures within the structures, seeking to explain what seem obsessive patterns, to grasp the interplay of writer and social process at deeper levels of consciousness. Because of its incisiveness, however, this method is necessarily incomplete. There are other obvious shaping forces at work in Clarke, factors at once narrower and broader, national and cultural in the widest sense of Western mind and myths. For Englishman Clarke, the Odyssey pattern has roots beyond social class or economic tensions. His native culture is not only strongly traditionalist, but also has a long tradition of explorers and explorations as well. As the geographic frontiers closed, new ones of the mind opened, and England became a pioneering nation in both technology and scientific speculation, the shaper of evolutionary vistas. It is easy to see how Odysseus, in his unique combination of adventurousness and insularity, would be an amenable hero to the English. The development of this heroic archetype remains, however, the work of Western civilization in general. It was the medieval Dante who first made of Homer's figure that restless seeker who foreshadowed the Renaissance. And it was this same international Renaissance, that, for all its boistrousness and daring, stressed the opposite impulse in the hero—the retreat to native hearth and family of Du-Bellay's *"heureux qui comme Ulysse a fait un beau voyage."* What nineteenth century England did was to reunite these two halves, and thus create an Odysseus who, if uniquely English and contemporary, remains nevertheless firmly anchored in the broader tradition.

At first glance there would appear no hero better suited to the technological nineteenth century than Odysseus—the crafty and practical prince willing to sacrifice even his name to get the job done. A rather different figure, however, emerges from Tennyson's poem "Ulysses"—weary, impotent, lamenting a heroic world that is no more. These two images are less disparate than they might seem. Tennyson's hero is a direct, organic outgrowth of the traditional figure, the old Ulysses caught up in new evolutionary vistas. Clearly, he is still the practical man of many experiences. But these begin to fade in what seems to be an ever-flattening future: "Yet all experience is an arch where through/Gleams that untravelled world whose margin fades/For ever and ever when I move." He is still the insatiable voyager ("I cannot rest from travel"), and yet he is now immobilized, an "idle king" by a "still hearth." The one adventure still possible is that of the imagination, but it too is strangely compromised: "And this gray spirit yearning in desire/To follow knowledge like a sinking star,/Beyond the utmost bound of human thought." In this poem the hero himself, hearth-bound and yet transcendent, is frozen at the utmost limit of human endeavor. In the entropic drift of this world, the growth pattern seems hopelessly inverted—the father is now child to the man, old Ulysses in his transcendent urge younger than Telemachus "centered in the sphere of common duties." It is here, at this extreme point, that Ulysses, famed for finding solutions, must act. He appears to restore balance: "Though much is taken, much abides." And yet what can abide? The poem ends with a similar formula where the balance seems this time tipped in man's favor: "Made weak by time and fate, but strong in will/To strive, to seek, to find, and not to yield." What we have here is less a stoic's credo than an exercise in self-conscious lyricism whose final accent is ambivalent—at once stasis and negation. Seen in an evolutionary perspective, things are still winding down: this row of heroic values issues into passivity; before the onslaught of time, both man and will must yield. As man passes though, for a brief instant he is home again: there are flickering memories of a dead heroic past—"the great Achilles whom we knew"—and the mourning voice that resurrects them.

One can find here another reflection of that same weary and impotent bourgeoisie, unwilling to give up its particular class heritage (this Ulysses remains very much the ideal Enlightenment man, his speculations and lamentations rooted in practical experience of lands and customs: "Much have I seen and known. . ."), and yet unable to impose its elitist values on a proletarian present or future (Ulysses turns disdainfully from Telemachus's attempts "by slow prudence to make mild a rugged people"). To trace every pattern to a same source seems, however, almost a compulsion for this mode of analysis. Indeed, the reflex may be less reductive than it is defensive, for the ideology behind such "explications" is itself sorely menaced by the world view of these bourgeois scientists. Obviously there are more than just economic facts here—the sweeping materialism of evolution all but overshadows the dialectical variety; and the limits of middle-class man, beside those of biological man, suddenly seem insignificant. Moreover, the "class" involved is a much narrower, more specific one—writers and intellectuals, men whose reaction is primarily literary and cultural. They protest not their own socioeconomic irrelevance as a group but that of the humanist tradition itself—it is in this direction that their "maximum consciousness" lies. To reverse this cultural entropy Tennyson, in his Ulysses poems, revived the archetypal voyager, setting this most human of heroes on a new "last" adventure, this time across the face of contemporary science itself.

Clarke shares with Tennyson a fascination with this archetype. Though direct references to the *Odyssey* become more numerous in his later works, a most significant one occurs in the early novel, *Against the Fall of Night* (1948): "Once more he [Alvin] was at peace, as ages ago an earlier wanderer had been when, lashed to the mast of his ship, he had heard the song of the Sirens die away across the wine-dark sea." Clarke isolates in this passage a seminal episode for all his heroes' voyages. With a clever trick Odysseus immediately thwarts the collective menace of the Sirens—he plugs his men's ears with wax. But if the physical ordeal is over before it begins, it in turn sets the stage for an adventure of the mind. Society recedes into a supportive role: in their deaf world the men are no longer a polity but an instrument that serves to sail the ship through dangerous waters. Tied to his mast, immobile and will-less before the overwhelming presence of the Sirens, Odysseus is still protected from it, the solitary hero at the center paradoxically free to explore the mysteries of their song. Prefigured here is the Time Traveller: with all the resources of his world equally behind him, he too remains securely anchored in it while taking his intellectual voyage beyond the utmost bounds of man's reign on Earth (thus the Sirens: "We know all things which shall be hereafter on the fecund Earth"). Odysseus's situation is fraught with the same contradictions that beset Wells's and Clarke's heroes. The Sirens' song mingles beauty and despair—if the possibility of transcendence attracts, the simultaneous certainty of personal destruction repels. The hero would act but can only lament ("my heart ached to hear them out")—this ultimate human feat is an almost totally passive one. All that remains of the traditional heroic resolve is a negative act—Odysseus has himself tied to the mast. There is, in our latter-day Siren-hearers, a similar constriction around a point. Held to his still hearth, Tennyson's Ulysses can only yearn that "something ere the end. . . may yet be done." Wells's Traveller twice must "clamber back" to the saddle of his machine and safety. Over and over Clarke's heroes seem to reenact this same drama of negative volition: Sherrard's scream, Falcon's descents, the twilight acts of feeble men at that extreme point where (like Odysseus engaging the Sirens while his ship is sailing home) the going out is simultaneously a return. It may seem in these recent Odysseys that the rich variey of experience of the original voyage has itself contracted and run down, until the rhythm of adventure (physical and intellectual) has become no more than a faint entropic tremor. The Siren episode, however, teaches the contrary: here the Odyssey pattern proves vast enough to embrace even the possibility of these modern close encounters with the superhuman or the void, and still carry the hero safely back home; Clarke's Alvin, like his illustrious ancestor, can "be at peace" again. In the search for submerged patterns, analysis a la Goldmann can go only part way. It does help us to see that Clarke's world view is "non-dialectical"; in his fiction progress is ever offset by retreat and transcendence by elegy. Only the Odyssey pattern shows us that these contradictions need not be "tragically" irreconcilable, the image of a social system hopelessly paralyzed. In reality the horns of this dilemma are the terms of what has been and still strives to be a creative polarity—the eminently human dynamic rooted in the archetypal voyages of Odysseus, reborn perhaps in the promise of those new adventures Bertrand Russell sees modern man building "on the firm foundation of unyielding despair."

Another stumbling block to Goldmann's Marxist-oriented structuralism is the fundamentally national and parochial nature of Clarke's Odyssean response. The dilemma of man in the increasingly alienating universes that modern science erects would seem a general one, arising naturally in all technologically advanced societies, and especially in those capitalist ones where such scientific visions have become enshrined as repressive myths. Yet it is interesting to note the relative absence of Wells's and Clarke's Odyssey pattern both in American SF and in the literary tradition that nourishes it. If economic class struggle were the principal shaping force, then one might expect similar patterns developing simultaneously in two nations so alike in their mode of capitalism as England and America. This has not happened. In American literature the relation of man to cosmos appears to trace quite different figures. The source of this difference probably lies in the widely divergent cultural traditions of the two nations, or rather the lack of a tradition in America. The archetypal American explorer-voyager is the homeless Ahab. The world of this hero is one of action, not elegy, of energy rather than entropy. In fact, Ahab's journey is not an evolutionary one at all, but rather a search for absolutes in an ahistorical, elemental realm. An uncharted and unchartable wilderness is given order and meaning not by cunning or scientific observation but by personal commitment—the individual yearning is vindicated not by retrieval of the human but by its sacrifice. Both Ahab and his crew are uprooted; for them there is no homecoming, only the voyage out, the encounter with mystery, and the leap into annihilation. The quest of this anti-Odysseus echoes that of his land-bound equivalent, the equally archetypal Ichabod Crane. On this new soil European tradition has degenerated into a "Sleepy Hollow." On his way through life Ichabod, the drifter, seeks to convert these ancestral holdings to liquid cash. He and Ahab are energizers, scourges of tradition and roots.

Evidence of a fundamental disparity in cultures comes from Clarke himself in his preface for a 1970 edition of *Against the Fall of Night*. He mentions two sources of inspiration—Stapledon's *Last and First Men* and John W. Campbell's "Twilight," a story obviously inspired by Wells's *Time Machine*—and tells of his attempts to sell his own novel to *Astounding*, thinking it was in Campbell's vein: "To my disappointment [he] turned it down. . . His main complaint was that it was too downbeat—though nothing could have been more downbeat than his own 'Twilight.' I incorporated some of his suggestions. . . but John remained dissatisfied." The reason for this misunderstanding seems to lie in the irreconciliability of Clarke's Odyssean vision to an American pattern whose coordinates are less tradition and evolution than grace and predestination. Though both writers owe a debt to the same seminal work, Campbell has altered the evolutionary voyage in significant ways. Once again, in "Twilight," a traveller goes through time to witness man's decline—he finds no Morlocks but a "dead city" of eternal machines, and living above it a race of feeble creatures, the vestiges of humanity. At this point elegy reappears, but its form and direction have changed. Here it is not the traveller but these last men who mourn: "And the songs. Those tell the story best. . . Little, hopeless, wondering men amid vast, unknowing blind machines that started three million years before." Their pathetic music in no way reasserts man's dignity before the indifferent universe. Campbell gives them a savior. His hero is "no ordinary man" in a very special sense—his tone is not elegaic but incantatory, messianic, his actions god-like. Unlike Wells's or Clarke's figures, he intervenes in the evolutionary process and actually suspends it, re-creating this world he has entered: "So I brought another machine to life. . . I ordered it to make a machine which would have what man had lost. A curious machine." What seems an evolutionary tale is more an allegory. Here is a fortunate fall with a twist, for if curiosity was once the primal sin, now it has become the essence of humanity, just as man is suddenly the measure of all things. To make this machine "curious" is to remake it in the image, not just of man, but of a special, technological man. In one stroke all pretense of evolutionary process vanishes before this act of intervening grace. A new super-race is created, but it is only because the machine finally gets a "soul"—a uniquely human one. In much cruder fashion, this same pattern occurs in George Pal's American film version of *The Time Machine*. The presence of grace is more blatantly obvious here. The Eloi are degenerate in a particular way—they lack curiosity, especially the kind which will lead them to act in behalf of a savior ("self-sacrifice"). Though fallen, they still dwell in the garden—the paradisical hull is there, only the energizing soul is lacking. The same is true of the Eloi's bodies—in their beauty original innocence remains visible. This chosen people await the "spark" the traveller—messiah beings—less the flame of Enlightenment exposing dark corners of superstition than a holy fire destroying the Morlock's dark Satanic mills, lifting the elect to instant glory. In the traveller's coming (what brings him to pull the lever of his vehicle and stop in the improbable yet crucial year of 802,701 A.D.?) technological knowledge and divine guidance are suddenly one. At the heart of the macrohistorical process one kind of man—the visionary engineer, physically unchanging throughout his travels—abides eternally as agent of some higher design. Here as in 'Twilight'' the evolutionary voyage is little more than a travesty: at the moment of grace all horizontal pretense falls away to reveal this static, vertical relationship between chosen individual and divinely ordained system.

Clarke's story in turn borrows things from Campbell, but it is only to place them in his native tradition. *Against the Fall* has the same eternal machine-city, the same twilight humanity. These details, however, are given an Odyssean twist. Clarke's hero Alvin, if he is special, is less the messiah than he is an "atavism"—in looking forward he simultaneously looks home-ward, back to the primitive roots of his race. To regenerate a world, he must turn to the past rather than the future—the name of his dead city, Diaspar, implies that the breach to be healed is a most ancient one. It is ironic that Clarke's tale, while it projects a far more genuine evolutionary panorama than Campbell's, is at the same time far less progressive. In Camp-bell the human element is reinfused at the end of time: super-man is created. Each successive stage of Alvin's Odyssey, however, ends with a spectacle of human passing that he is powerless to change: the voyage to Lys ends in Shalmirane with its dying Watcher and never-to-return Great Ones, while his journey to the stars terminates in the ruins of the once-great Empire. The people of the Empire have gone on to new gala-xies, only to discover new limits and desolation there. In each of these cases, in fact, what seemed a journey to some greater human future turns out (at the same time) to be a return to man's past. At Shalmirane Alvin discovers the Great Ones who, in the Odyssean perspective, are at one and the same time "a mystery from the stars" and a relic of his own past. In the same way, the advanced civilization he discovers near the Central Sun turns out to be but another ruin of past human glory. Expecting the strange, he comes upon a world very like his own: " 'This planet was dry as Earth,' he said dully." The history of the Empire obeys this same rhythm: they who have gone on are now returning from their exodus to the old home on Earth. What must have struck Campbell as "down-beat" here is this endless constriction, for Clarke's hero (and behind him all mankind) remains Odysseus tied to his mast, observing but never intervening, all the while being carried back to his roots. The present is not (as in the elliptical leaps of Campbell's or Pal's travellers) abandoned for the future, but remade in terms of the past and tradition. In uniting city with garden, Alvin grounds his society firmly in unchanging rhythms—natural but controlled—just as Odysseus did when he reduced the wild forces of nature and man to the tree-bed. In turn one can see what Clarke saw as "downbeat" in Camp-bell's story, with its latent Calvinism which supplants tradition-al and representative man with elect man. Clarke's later response to these super-machines is Howard Falcon. However curious or superior, a machine remains a machine here: if Falcon falls the very moment he rises, it is because of his very human hubris. But if this later Clarkean elegy at man's passing seems to give way to irony at the expense of his tenacity, or to this all-too-human need to hold fast as the center of creation, one question is still to be heard: what or who can replace a man? To Clarke's English humanist tradition the question is fundamental. By constantly asking it, his fiction is able to pass safely between the Scylla and Charybdis of Campbell's American vision—annihilation and transcendence, or more accurately, damnation and salvation.

If transcendence seems promised in Stapledon—the other source of inspiration Clarke names—it serves a very different function: here is a force which does not suspend the Odyssey pattern so much as stretch its field of action. Once again a comparison with an American writer—this time Le Guin, whose Hainish are in a very real sense the equivalent of Stapledon's last and first men—will help to set these divergent cultural visions in relief. At first glance Le Guin's fictional universe might appear to obey the Odyssean dynamic. From novel to novel her Hainish universe is expanding and progressing. Opposing this forward movement is a counterthrust: gradually the mystery of this race—the source of all development— deepens until we wonder where the farthest shore of Le Guin's universe really lies, in the future or in the past. Her latest novel, *The Dispossessed*, faces this problem of direction squarely. For its hero, Shevek, the adventure—"crossing the line" or going out—is at the same time a coming home: Urras is his ancestral planet. This voyager (in seemingly Odyssean fashion) is even more essentially a voyager of the mind. He confronts the same paradoxical rhythm of time on the theoretical plane: the solution to the sequency—simultaneity controversy is to choose both—succession and cotemporality, past and future—as they meet at the crossroads of his own human existence. However familiar this landscape may seem, it is navigated in a radically different manner. Shevek's return home is actually a discovery, not that his home is no more, but that it never was: in the relativistic universe he discovers there can be no home in the physical sense, no fixed place or unyielding physical roots in tradition. Although apparently solid things are cut loose, and the terms forward and backward suddenly made meaningless, it is so that a new solid center may be found. At the core of the novel Shevek has what is clearly a mystical experience: "At this instant the difference between this planet and that one. . . was no more significant to him than the difference between two grains of sand. . . There was no more exile. He had seen the foundations of the universe, and they were solid." The only anchor at this moment of revelation is the consciousness of Shevek himself. More than simple discovery of an order, Shevek's new awareness of self leads literally to an act of world creation. The currents which fuse at this individual point of vision are both multiple and rootless: "Ainsetain's" homeless theory of relativity, Shevek's natural home on Urras set against his ideological one on Anarres. This chaos takes shape: the hero, with his new sense of purpose beyond the paradoxes of time/space, invents the "ansible," the simultaneous communication device that will make the later League (already the reader's fictional past) possible. In both cases the physical event does not precede this epiphany but follows it *ex nihilo*. Here the elegaic movement of Stapledon's or Clarke's men is exactly reversed. For with these writers, even if there can be no return to a physical homeland, there is always a return to some immutable idea relating to it.

For all Shevek's gropings after an answer, it appears to come unbidden. His illumination also triggers in Ketho the Hainishman another, apparently wider one: "We have been civilized for a thousand millennia. . . we have tried everything. . . But I have not tried it. They say there is nothing new under the sun. But if each life is not new, each single life, then why are we born?" In this vertical suspension of "I" and "we," past and future, those same last and first men that Stapledon strings out across evolutionary time are suddenly disengaged from the processes of history and biology. What we have here is less evolution than grace. Behind the apparent democratic urge spurring this demand that "each single life" be freed from the constraints of time and place lies a restriction of a different, higher order: all men must be open to this possible revelation of uniqueness so that the unknown few who are chosen can receive it. In this novel they are two—Ketho and Shevek—men not so much born as born again. As he acts on the Hainishman the hero appears to be the agent of a destiny which, rather than preserve that common humanity whose powers and limits the Odyssean man represents, elevates special men instead. The promised transcendence in Stapledon or Clarke is essentially collective in nature. In Le Guin, however, it is selective, its action effecting a qualitative separation very much like that between elect and damned. Before this secularized grace the

33

pageant of human progress or decline fades, as illusion before the light of revealed truth.

Certainly these samplings are too few to define national traditions. But they do indicate irreconcilable differences of approach to the common problem of man and scientific vision, tradition and biological "destiny." Stapledon's transcendent mysticism seems to be leading Clarke further away from a stricter Wellsian view of evolution toward the teleology of *Childhood's End* and *2001*, in which movement toward other or "higher" states of being comes from an outside pull rather than any sort of "drive" within. In neither writer is the Odyssey pattern overthrown: always at the point of transcendence man passes and is retrieved. *Last and First Men*, however extended its panorama, ends with a similar confrontation of cosmic indifference and elegy—man's "brief music" in which "despair wakens into peace." Behind the Last Man's song lies the protracted lament of a century of English poetry facing the increasingly unhuman vistas of scientific speculation: Tennyson's "Lotus-Eaters" with its weary Ulysses and entropic landscape—twin visions of lost home and impossible transcendence echoing back and forth at each other in one long choric lament. The Romantic nightingale becomes Hardy's Darkling Thrush, "flinging his soul upon the glowing gloom." Human and natural energies ebb away in Arnold, and the seas of "Dover Beach" recede to leave that same cold, silent shore on which Wells's Traveller finally comes to rest. Like all these, the last lines of Stapledon's even more elegaic *Last Men in London* reverberate through all of Clarke's work: "Man, a moth sucked into a furnace, vanishes; and then the furnace also, since it is but a spark islanded in the wide, the everlasting darkness. If there is a meaning, it is no human meaning. Yet one thing in all this welter stands apart, unassailable, fair, the blind recollection of past light." Here in quintessential form is the pattern: man disappears ("too soon he comes to his end") and yet like Shelley's Adonais is preserved: "eternally a beauty in the eternal form of things." Star or star-child, the pattern of retrieval remains the same. Because of its deep ties to a native tradition that is ultimately more lyrical than narrative, Clarke's fiction (like that of Wells and Stapledon before him) is more than a "literature of ideas," either in the traditional sense or in the hidden one the Goldmann school seeks. In their strange mixture of epic and lyric elements, his "novels" plunge their generic roots elsewhere, deep in the Homeric paradigm whose

structural possibilities (in Protean fashion) elude narrow

categorization. In fact, it is to British SF that we must turn—to Clarke's space odysseys—to have the latest sea change of this hero who is also a poet, the first voyager on the edges of human possibility.

SIX ODYSSEYS

To be useful in criticism, general patterns must pass the practical test: does the search for this "Odyssey pattern" in individual novels of Clarke impoverish them, or does it open their respective meaning structures to increasingly subtle and flexible analysis? The second part of this essay confronts the pattern with six novels chosen from all periods of Clarke's activity. These have been purposely selected at random in hopes that they will thus offer maximum resistence to any preconceived idea of order. They do, however, fall roughly into categories: early, middle, and later Clarke. Novels like *The Sands of Mars* (1951) and *Islands in the Sky* (1952), in spite of their dates of publication, actually plunge their roots into the '40s and the American magazine SF of that period. Less "primitive" is a work like *Childhood's End* (1953), where Clarke in one big step seems to have moved away from the manipulation of space opera conventions toward Odyssean adventure that is openly in the speculative manner of Wells. What appears evolutionary is actually parallel development: this strain too, with the early *Against the Fall of Night*, reaches back into the '40s. If during this formative period the young writer seems to hover between Campbell and Stapledon, he quickly chooses the latter, and evolutionary drama replaces pulp adventure in the novels of Clarke's middle period—the later '50s and '60s. If *Childhood's End* is Clarke's first major Odyssean adventure, *2001: A Space Odyssey* (1968)—whatever Kubrick's role in its creation—remains his most classic. Indeed, the fact that it is an omnibus work, composed consciously and laboriously out of various short pieces from this middle period, may account for its linear purity, its almost literal self-awareness of the pattern it develops. This self-conscious stance becomes more obvious in Clarke's two novels of the '70s: *Rendezvous with Rama* (1973) and *Imperial Earth* (1976). In spirit these works seem to turn away from the elegaic mysticism of Clarke's middle period back toward the creative vision of the earliest pulp-inspired novels. Both are aware of a set of conventions as manipulable counters; both weave increasingly intricate and personal figures out of them. This time, however, the raw material is more sophisticated—not the cliches of the juveniles but the Odyssey pattern itself. The goal of this fictional game seems far different in these latest novels—no longer neutral analysis of man's condition so much as pointed satire against his foibles and follies.

Before discussing the individual novels, a problem must be raised: how are we to judge their literary value? This remains the Achilles heel of Goldmann's method. In one breath the critic claims "scientific" objectivity for his method: the general pattern is tested against specific works. In the next, because works do not write themselves, he finds it necessary to weight his conclusions with old aphorisms such as "greatness." His argument is thoroughly circular: the "great" writer is he whose work is most "coherent"; coherence in turn is defined as "maximum consciousness"; this consciousness, however, turns out to be more a qualitative than a quantitative factor—the perception of certain historical dynamics as Marx defined them. Greatness has to do less with literary factors than extra-literary goals. However coherent Clarke's structural vision may be, because it cultivates antitheses rather than seeking to resolve them, it is blind—a tragic opacity to even more tragic inconsistencies in his society. A writer thus "unaware" automatically is not a great writer. Within this system mediocrity receives swift and awful punishment: because he cannot understand it, Clarke is damned in Sisyphean manner to repeat his pattern endlessly.

Gerard Klein's judgment of SF, though its ultimate appeal is also to "genius," is more interesting: "The conditions are perhaps present for the writing of a new *Don Quixote* in the field of SF. All that remains is to find Cervantes." Though Klein is referring mainly to socioeconomic consciousness, his example invokes purely literary standards as well: greatness is the awareness of contending conventions, the ability to fuse them into new revolutionary structures. But even here, in this apparently neutral realm of literary process, judgment is hazardous. Another distinction, that of Jean Rousset between "formula" and "form," is equally value-weighted. Ostensibly "formula" refers to literary and cultural patterns in historical limbo, "form" to the fusion of those patterns into works of art through interaction with the individual creative mind. It is implied here that only great writers create "forms"—the circle begins again. Thus Clarke may become increasingly conscious of his Odyssey pattern, but does he shape its contending strains, elevating it to form? The search for an answer may lead to more concrete perceptions: the shift from elegy to satire in his latest novels, for instance, may not mark an advance but rather deeper retreat into formulaic response to man's condition in the scientific age. Ultimately, however, the matter is decided by subjective impulse—Clarke simply is not Cervantes. This study tries at least to suspend such comparisons and merely to describe Clarke's attempt to fuse traditional patterns and current dilemmas. In this way, even if it is conceded in the end that science fiction is still waiting for its great shaper, Clarke's work may nevertheless tell us something about why we wait.

However derivative novels like *The Sands of Mars* and *Islands in the Sky* may seem on the surface, they are surprisingly original creations, and in their structural dynamics already thoroughly Clarkean. Their originality does not lie in the larger narrative patterns—these are stock juvenile or "adult" space adventure—but rather in the way in which these conventional structures are subordinated to a persistent intellectual framework. Informing and reshaping the familiar cliches and themes everywhere in these two novels is an embryonic form of the Odyssey pattern. In both, a perfectly bland surface map is drawn—as readers of SF our conventional expectations would lead us blindfolded over its contours—only to be dotted with numerous and unexpected points of encounter with cosmic mystery. "Drama" lies less in resolution of plot than in a cumulation of these moments of tension between man and material limits. In these novels too—though in ways more often humorous than ponderous—man is constantly suspended at the crossroads between transcendent possibility and the pull of his lost home. What is really unique here is not so much the fact that Clarke uses "entertaining" genres—juvenile and space operas—to make more serious investigations, as the manner in which he proceeds and the inflection he gives these investigations. His attitude is essentially playful, analytical in a detached sense. In other, later novels the problem will not change—it is ever the human condition—but only the writer's stance: the mode of analysis passes from cerebral to elegaic, and finally to ironic. If Clarke's latest novels appear to come full circle to these stylized games with the convention of the beginning, it is with a different accent: the late Clarke shades toward the satirical, while these early tales are pure arabesque.

Of these two period novels, *The Sands of Mars* bears the earlier date. It seems, however, both by virtue of its "adult" theme (the space writer takes his maiden voyage into space) and the leisurely, almost reflective treatment of that theme, somehow less patently derivative of pulp SF than its companion, *Islands in the Sky*. On the surface, in fact, *Islands* seems just another juvenile adventure of the sort codified by Heinlein. Indeed, its "plot" can be resumed in terms of stock Heinleinian elements. The hero, young Roy Malcolm, is the typical "wise" lad of convention: he wins his "jackpot to space" by exploiting a legal loophole in the quiz-show prize he is given, and ends up quoting interplanetary law to a befuddled MC. Roy's Mom and Dad are the conventional stick-close-to-Earth parents (the former is predictably foolish and prissy, as befits the Heinleinian housewife: " '*I* don't whirl stones on the ends of strings,' said Mom, 'and I hope you won't either, at least not indoors.' "); but Roy is egged on by the familiar bachelor uncle-as-visionary, Uncle Jim. To get into space, Roy must undergo the stock medical *rite de passage*. Once clear he takes off on a rolling-stone tour of the various communications satellites that orbit this Earth of the not-too-distant future, meeting with the conventional mixture of adventure, horseplay, and education or character formation. There is the usual assortment of peer-types (Karl Hasse the humorless mathematical "genius," Ronnie Jordan the space bully—names with roles but no human substance); there seems to be the usual string of adventures, with a predictable alteration of comic and "serious" outcomes: the meeting with the "hydra" at the space hospital ends in comedy, while the plunge toward the moon is a near-tragedy. Finally, there is the ubiquitous mentor figure—here the legless Captain Doyle—who watches over the hero as he passes through his apparently fortuitous string of adventures, and singles him out in the end as one of the elite—the happy few fit for "space duty." With a typical flourish, Roy returns to Earth wiser, better, and a man, vowing he will "go out again."

The reader of the novel perceives these cliches as through a distorting lens, rearranged or refocused by an ordering principle operating beneath (and often against) the visible plot line. An example of this refocusing technique is Clarke's use of the old device of ship names. We have two here with particular resonances: the *Skylark* and the *Morning Star*. These names do not function (as they would in Heinlein) in a linear manner, as extensions of a "heroic" past into some open-ended space future. Instead, they act as points of confrontration between literary fable and material reality, between human aspirations and devouring time. The *Skylark* is not the great interstellar ship of myth, but a lowly space shuttle. And if the *Morning Star* made history on the first Venus run, now it is only an obsolete cadets' training vessel. When pressed into service again by an emergency, it does not assault the heavens, but merely transfers a patient to the space hospital—this bold act of mercy is by space adventure standards a milk run. Nothing, however, moves in a straight line in Clarke's universe, neither upward *ad astra* nor downward in an endless string of deflations. Clarke here is not systematically undermining the heroic so much as using these contrasts as the means of exploring the protean nature of human existence. The *Morning Star* should (were it to live up to its name) take a heroic voyage—it takes a routine one instead. This, however, turns out to be an adventure after all: as the boys head off course and drift into space the danger is real, not romanticized.

In *Islands* Clarke has retained the old pulp device of the ''cliff-hanger'' chapter which he reinforces (in typical juvenile fashion) with catching captions or titles (''A Plague of Pirates''). And yet by constantly balancing these conventional points of suspense against moments of discovery that are basically contemplative in nature, he creates a curious counterpoint, undercutting the traditional modes of surprise with new surprises of his own. These moments of discovery are clearly Odyssean in nature: all at once the strange or uncanny occurs in the commonplace; or the transcendent menace is suddenly reversed, spilled back into the familiar and comfortable. Such moments may coincide with a crest of physical adventure; more often, however, they fall in a trough, at some negative or aheroic point of physical immobility. An example of this first kind of counterpoint, where Odyssean tensions are played off against conventional patterns of adventure, is the ''hydra'' episode. The first surprise coincides exactly with the juvenile formula: in the routine setting of the space hospital the boys open a door, encountering darkness and mystery in the form of what they think to be a great tentacular monster. A sudden ''flood of light'' resolves all—the ''hydra'' is only a harmless if overgrown plant. We learn at the same time that this is no Venusian plant, but in reality a microscopic organism from Earth increased to huge proportions because of weightlessness. In true Odyssean fashion the voices of science and reason reveal only stranger disorientations, for they cannot explain away our malaise at this transformation of the commonplace. And if the idea of relativity is of little help here, neither is that of evolution. Here in space the familiar has become alien, but that alien constantly yearns to return to the familiar. This is clearly seen in the case of the man from Mars, whom the boys save on 39 their mercy mission. He too is a displaced growth—on Mars he has become inadapted to Earth gravity, and like the monstrous plant can never return. In Clarke's universe things seem to be evolving inexorably forward (the plant now belongs in space, the patient's home now *is* Mars); at the same time, they constantly regress as well. The boys name this organism a "hydra"—to accept it they must domesticate it to their mythology. The patient too, separated from his familiar world by a biological chasm, takes a telescope and gazes back at Earth and those lost "green hills" of space opera elegy.

Roy's first "space walk," on the other hand, is an example of a moment of discovery that cuts squarely across the juvenile adventure framework, so that the contrast of expectations helps elevate what would remain a filler situation to a level of mystical intensity. Here is one of Clarke's frozen moments—a point where opposites are held in tense suspension, maximum inertia giving rise to furthest penetration. As in a mirror, Roy looks down on the familiar world of Earth's Congo from this new world where "up" and "down" no longer have meaning. This Congo was not always so familiar: yet those explorers Roy evokes—Stanley and Livingstone—are reflected in this new explorer who is also a boy on a paid vacation. All sense of direction is suddenly lost, the evolutionary process (Livingstone to Roy, Africa to outer space) suspended in this confrontation of likes that are at the same time profoundly unlike—we are faced with progress and decadence all at once, man's surge forward simultaneously offset by his slide backward. What is more, this moment is immediately reinforced by another, even more clearly Odyssean situation. At the end of his tether Roy turns to look, not into deep space, but back to Earth, only to find that the familiar has become strange, the home world of light a thing of darkness: "There was the great black shield of Earth, no, not quite black, for I could see the oceans glimmering in the moonlight. The same light made the slim girders around me gleam like the threads of a ghostly spider's web. . . This was the moment when I really knew that I had reached space at last, and that nothing else could ever be the same again." Here it seems the familiar must become alien so that Earth and space can be joined by this very Keatsian moonlight that enfolds opposites in a common beauty. Yet this moment of union is also one of profound separation—Roy now knows he is in space, he has changed and can't go home again. Ironically, though, as he faces his new world, this is exactly what he is doing: Tim is hauling in his life-line all the while; like

40

his ancestor Odysseus before the Sirens, he is being drawn inexorably home. In a sense this Inner Station functions here as a kind of Calypso's isle in reverse. The Homeric island is far from home on one narrative level (how the story is told), yet on another (the story itself) it is actually quite near. Clarke's station may be physically close to Earth, but in terms of Roy's voyage it is a far point; for though later events may take the hero to more distant geographical places, these remain detours, part of a protracted homecoming. The space walk is almost emblematic of this Odyssean paradox. After long inactivity on this island the ancient adventurer is suspended momentarily between Calypso and Penelope—the supernatural and the domestic. The attraction of the former is not less—he admits she is more beautiful. Nor is his choice of the latter wholly conscious—at the moment of decision the divine machinery is in motion, Odysseus is already on his way home. Roy's position in space is analogous, for if he feels the Romantic mystery of these magic casements, at the same time a very real force is drawing him in the opposite direction homeward.

In *Islands*, elaboration of these paradoxes of direction reaches its high point at the "In the Abyss" chapter, where the boys, after their flight to the space hospital in the *Morning Star* (a trip supposedly fraught with danger but actually without the least incident), are heading calmly home in a new vessel. The basic out-and-back pattern of this microcosmic episode again serves only as a frame against which a complex series of directional shifts are woven. Set against this routine homecoming is Doyle's tale of going out—his account of the Mercury exploration. If Roy's earlier encounter with the "hydra" is mock-heroic, Doyle's meeting with the rock-throwing Mercurian is serious and analogous to Odysseus's Cyclops adventure in interesting ways. In the ancient poem the Cyclops's inhospitability was a moral failing. Here, however, the situation is redirected: the Mercurian is not a degradation of the human form but on the contrary a triumph of the evolutionary process, a creature perfectly adapted to a world hostile to man. What is more, he cripples Doyle not from malice but "for survival." Doyle nevertheless remains hurt, paralyzed at the limits of human possibility. As he looks out on the aurora, its beauty and grandeur are offset by his physical weakness, the attraction outward by the pull back—the frozen man must be carried away from these cosmic lights to his ship and home. In *Islands* the counterweight to an indifferent universe comes less from elegy—Doyle's lyrical perception is the briefest spark—than from the contrived dynamics of the fictional machine itself. In this novel man never really reaches his absolute end; rather, he is caught in a seemingly endless web of reversals. Thus, while we experience Doyle's predicament on Mercury, we know he is not really there, but sitting in the comfort of his homebound ship. That home, we suddenly realize, cannot be Roy's familiar Earth, for the effects of this Mercurian voyage—his leglessness—have made Doyle a permanent exile in space. And even here, this comfort he presently enjoys will also prove elusive. For though he thinks they are heading back, his ship is actually (because of a navigational error) heading in the opposite direction, out into space. All aboard may experience far reaches of fear, but physically their path will have little thrust. The "death ship" they meet turns out to be a relic of Earth's past—radioactive wastes. And if their cosmos is only a garbage dump, their odyssey succumbs to a routine refueling from a now well-domesticated moon.

This comparison between Roy's adventures and Doyle's is by no means fortuitous, for Clarke's structure forces these unlikely opposites—seasoned hero and groping novice—into mirror suspension. Indeed, the respective trajectories of these two protean existences cross and balance each other in almost chiasmic fashion. Though immobilized on Mercury, Doyle takes his farthest voyage—an odyssey of mind and spirit. On the homebound ship things are exactly reversed—he is totally in command yet blind, unaware that the ship itself has been turned completely around. To complicate matters even more, Roy as apprentice and stowaway follows a path analagous to Doyle's, but reversed. The "Abyss" chapter begins not with Roy seeing but with him blacking out. His dream, induced by oxygen-starvation, may parallel Doyle's moment of delirium on Mercury, but again the thrust is opposite. Doyle looks not back but out—his vision is one of grandeur. Roy in his dream returns to the familiar world of Inner Station only to find the known suddenly distorted into nightmare. Dazzled by the heavenly fires, Doyle is destroyed unawares, numbed and frozen. Roy on the other hand, though his dream is one of violent dismemberment (he sees himself sucked into a ventilator fan), awakens to find himself not a cripple but a savior ("After all I *had* acted as a sort of human guinea pig to warn the others."). These opposing life lines may seem to meet at a common center—this passivity of the heroic moment. If so, the balance is again a Janus-face, the crisscrossing of contrary impulses. Even as Doyle looks out into the mysteries of space, he is being physically carried home. In contrast Roy, on this routine shuttle flight, looks out of the porthole homeward, only to discover an unexpected marvel—an Earth getting smaller, not bigger. The apprentice may replace the commander as seer-hero here—Doyle is blind, Roy "the only one who noticed" the ship had turned around. But though they move in opposite directions, each is being carried. Whatever balance then exists in the universe of *Islands* comes not from men's acts but from their situation, as focus of this rhythm of simultaneous voyage and return.

But if man in this novel remains passive in the face of larger forces, these are clearly not evolutionary in nature. The thing which controls events here is the principle of polarity—the ceaseless play of opposites that shapes a world at once protean and rigorously structured, changing yet static. This rhythm finds symbolic embodiment in the planet Mercury. It is a place of symmetrical surprises. Though men make incredible discoveries (life seems impossible yet exists), the physical landscape of the planet is itself virtually unmoving: "One side is in perpetual darkness, the other in blazing light." Indeed the incredible "darkside" creature himself incarnates this same polar dynamic: white body for minimum heat loss, black wings (the planet is airless) to absorb heat. Even mystery is ordered here, for if we don't know what that fearful Mercurian from the sun side might look like, we do know he would be the product of exactly opposite conditions. Mercury then is more than a lesson in evolutionary ecology. It is rather an organizing pattern that echoes across the whole novel. The planet binds hot and cold, light and darkness. It is both the innermost world and Doyle's farthest shore. In like manner Roy goes to Inner Station only to plunge into the wonders of space. And if his adventure is overshadowed by Doyle's, the commander's longest voyage turns out to be coexistent with the novel's most static moment— the telling of the tale. All across the apparently linear surface of this space adventure objects and actions condense into nodes of contradiction—opposite impulses joined in what could be called Odyssean conceits.

In like manner the classic Heinleinian ending is neutralized as well. The hero does indeed come home, only to decide he will go out again—now is the time for the stars. This resolve to go to Mars is offset by the family of "Martians" he meets travelling in the opposite direction—earthward. To the Moores, Roy's home is an alien land (even physically they can no longer function in its gravity). Yet as humans it is their home 43 too. Doyle with no legs is permanently exiled in space (and as such—like the later Howard Falcon—gains new capabilities only at the expense of the old form), but the Moores have only sea legs—they can readapt, sink roots. This time, as Roy puts on the Martian clothes his new friends offer him, the focal point of two opposing lines becomes the human form itself. As with the Moores, Roy will be simultaneously at home and yet alien on both worlds. His rediscovery of Earth's weather overlaps with the revelation of Martian meterology, in which the everyday is most wondrous—electrical storms without clouds. But the return to Earth is also marked with strangeness-in-familiarity: "It was an eerie sound, and it made the hair rise at the back of my neck. . . at the speed we were traveling even the incredibly thin atmosphere. . . was protesting as we tore through it." And if now, in a new reversal, Roy decides to overleap Doyle and Inner Station for Mars, it is only to strike a new balance, where voyage and homecoming again coincide. If the Moores seek roots on Earth, Roy finds that man's future on Mars may in reality be a past. The novel ends less with the traditional defiance of the heavens than with the lyrical evocation of a Martian civilization tht may be "more ancient than ours." Exploration then has become archeology, evolution little more than reaffirmation of the static center of tradition.

The young hero of *Islands* may seem more a Telemachus than an Odysseus. Roy's blood parents do not understand him, but in the end he finds his true father in Commander Doyle and his roots in space, on a Mars that is at once strange and familiar, alien yet traditional. In *The Sands of Mars* this father-son relationship is even more central to the action. This time however, the perspective is turned around—the hero is an adult, an Odysseus. It is this pattern which here, in this novel, transforms narrative structures again borrowed from pulp SF. Clarke has added to the ever-present space voyage another familiar theme: the adult's discovery of a meaningful existence on a pioneer world. The theme lies behind all of Heinlein's "adults"—give a man a role worthy of him and he will rise to it. Clarke's variant in *Sands* is the "space writer" who finally confronts the realities of space. Shaping the cliche to its own particular ends is the Odyssean pattern—a son's education will lead to the discovery both of father and ordered world, of old home and new home. In fact, there is here, as in *The Odyssey*, a double discovery: a boy finds his father, and that father in turn finds his own parent in the end, in the strangest manner possible, and on a strange world suddenly become home.

Once again the basic form of the narrative is a voyage out and back—this time to Mars. And here too the official destination is not necessarily the farthest shore: there is a possibility of encounter with the infinite at any point, near or far. The framing formula is again reversed into an Odyssean world: not the main voyage but these secondary adventures become the true focus of interest. In *Sands* Clarke makes much more elaborate use of the "space-walk" device. Martin Gibson, the writer-snooper on his way to Mars, is lured from his room (a meteor hole must be fixed without his knowledge) by being taken for a turn in space. This routine bit of tourism once more becomes a moment of dizzying vision: "That misty spectre was a million times farther away than the stars. . . How pitiful were all men's voyagings and adventures when seen against this background!" This vastness is suddenly balanced against a strange "white rectangular object floating against the stars" which turns out to be nothing less than one of his own manuscript pages ("Nothing could have been more commonplace— or more unexpected here"). Earlier, as he sped away from Earth, Gibson found that a thumbnail suffices to blot out all of man's home world: "Soon I shall be able to eclipse with my little finger what was, until a lifetime ago, all of Man's dominion and everything that his art had saved from time." Things now are turned around: it is space that blots out man, the writer unable to grasp its overwhelming power in words. Yet at this moment the lone sheet of paper takes on new significance: "When he had been dead for ages, that piece of paper would still be carrying its message out among the stars; and what it was, he would never know." Out of these almost abstract patterns of reversal (man as god or man as mote) a new elegiac confrontation seems to be emerging here—the pathetic fragility of the human voice isolated against the indifferent heavens. This white dot is not even a finished work, merely a draft; it remains nonetheless the voice of art, enduring as it strikes an impossible balance with the void.

As in *Islands* an adventure is narrated at the heart of this novel which again reaches far beyond the physical limits of the story itself. If Hilton's tale also carries us to the extremes of human endurance, the direction this time is not toward the sun but away from it, to the "Ultima Thule" of Saturn's moons. This narrator, however, speaks with a slightly different tone. Initially Hilton is calm and detached ("But it was a different thing to hear Hilton. . . as if he had been a spectator rather than a participant"). Unlike Doyle he has experienced alien beauties without suffering physical violence or direct harm. The only thing that seems to move him is the thought of returning to Saturn. As he speaks of it, he lapses into lyrical accents that echo Tennyson's world-weary Ulysses: "And I want to land on Mimas again, and see that great shining crescent reaching half way up the sky. . . " Hilton has gone beyond deeds to become the contemplative hero at the point where deeds are futile. What is more, his Saturnian tale is juxtaposed in mood and mode to the equally static narrative situation which contains it: the Martian explorers have crashed in the planet's desert. Out of this juxtaposition a series of ironic contrasts emerges. Here as on Saturn the physical danger of adventure evaporates—the men swap stories in a heated ship and wait for certain rescue. But the apparently known world outside suddenly turns out to be as strange as the faraway moons: life on Mars is deemed impossible, yet they find it. This fantastic discovery will in turn lead back to something more familiar: Mars will get a breathable atmosphere, becoming more like Earth. Yet we need only turn this familiar image slightly, and, like the chameleon Martian, it appears strange again. The Martian may fit into patterns of human relationship but it is not human: "Three people had gone into the forest; but four were coming out. And the fourth looked a very odd sort of person indeed." Plants on Mars are like ours and yet not—they are both heliotropic and flowerless.

Home is an even more ambiguous concept in *Sands*—a place at once rooted and adrift. Throughout this novel man seems to be pressing forward. But here again conquest of the future seems to coincide with a return to the past: if man inhabits new worlds, it is only to discover their profound attachment with the old. In leaving Earth Gibson believes he severs all ties cultural and biological: "Down there is all my past life, and the lives of all my ancestors back down to the first blob of jelly in the first primeval sea." His voyage out, however, is ironically a voyage back. Human bonds that no longer exist on troubled, over-sophisticated Earth are rediscovered. The "space writer" confronts real spacemen, and finds himself in a world (however microscopic) of true human relationships: "It was curious to think that before the voyage had ended, he would probably know every one of them better than most of his acquaintances back on Earth. There could be. . . no masks aboard the tiny world of the *Ares*." Gibson's remark about the virgin passenger quarters on the ship—"A house so new that no one has ever lived in it can be more lonely than an old, deserted ruin that has once known life and may still be peopled by ghosts."—applies to his new home on Mars as well. These settlements are haunted by "ghosts" that are both Martian and human—tenacious yet complementary pasts. To Earth science the view that the Martians are degenerate survivors of some lost superior race is "romantic." But what is this revival of Earth society on Mars but a romantic return to the primitive—to a pioneer spirit long dead and to a garden world however strange. In both cases this is not a new race but a reborn one. In their present climb up the "evolutionary ladder" they seem to interact with each other. If man is responsible for making the planet bloom, it is only because he learned a lesson from the Martians and their plants. And man in turn will entrust the seeding of the planet—not as in Bradbury's *Martian Chronicles* to some new Johnny Appleseed—but to the Martians themselves.

Nevertheless, the basic pattern that controls this interplay remains one that is profoundly human and traditional—the relationship of father and son. Gibson's biggest discovery on this new world is that of Jimmy, his lost natural son. This discovery is only the core of a web of corresponding family ties on all levels of the narrative. Indeed, the relation of Mars to Earth plays a key role in this family drama. To Gibson Mars is both home and not home, for even if family ties not possible on Earth are discovered there, the family cannot take root in this soil. Gibson's act of self-fulfillment—his choice to stay on Mars—means he must be separated from Jimmy, who has to complete his studies on Earth if he is ever to return to the Red Planet. The two worlds then, paradoxically, find themselves even more closely linked by this fundamentally human pattern of separation. Gibson's choice, though it loses him a son, gains him the father he never had—the Martian Chief Executive Hadfield whom he is ultimately to succeed. By staying he gets a second son as well—this time a real Martian instead of the human variety—the young Squeak, who in unexplained fashion and against all laws of evolution (the other creatures show no curiosity or interest in humans) literally adopts Gibson. More significantly, Gibson's link to these two "sons" is paralleled by that of Mars to her two moons. When describing how "Operation Dawn" transformed Phobos into a ball of fire, Clarke permits a pun which underscores this relationship: "Though Mars had lost a moon it had gained a sun." This attempt to associate Gibson and Mars, thus to merge man and alien world, is reinforced in a more subtle manner by Jimmy's own moment of dawning as he takes leave of the older man to return to Earth: "It could have been the dawn of the first puzzled surmise, the birth of the still half-conscious thought that might grow at last to fully fledged understanding and recognition." At this crowning Odyssean moment—the mask of the familiar falls to reveal something at once more real and incredible—word-play too seems to blend with reality. The final balance that emerges is a stunning reversal: son as sun has become father to the new man of Mars.

This web of correspondences does not stop here. As the moons are to Mars, so Mars is to Earth, a rebellious son breaking away from its parent. What may seem merely an intricate game of surface relationships has in fact deeper significance. In this tale of space pioneers the ultimate irony is not that movement is suspended, but that through these suspensions it actually drifts backward. At the core of these relativizing comparisons there is an absolute—home remains Earth. Gibson can never be fully Martian, for as Norden warns him: "Don't forget that everything you've got here is due to the enterprise and initiative of Earth." And though man creates new suns, the old one dominates as source of that order and energy that both informs and transforms Mars. The Martians may seem protean, but their patterns of change are clearly controlled by the sun: "You see, they're always brown. . . on the side toward the sun." What is more, the sun directs the rhythm of the new man-made planet as well. As Gibson stands in the light of Mars's two "suns"—Phobos setting in the east as old Sol rises—he casts two shadows: "Both shadows pointed to the west, but though one scarcely moved, the fainter lengthened even as he watched, becoming more and more difficult to see, until at last it was snuffed out as Phobos dropped down behind the edge of Mars." The promise of advancement (westward the course of empire) is not only suspended here as the two planets turn in opposite directions; it is borne backwards. Clarke seems to build his own variation here on Plato's allegory of the cave. Progress is shadow, and man's efforts to conquer a new world have merely lit a lamp, brief and unnatural. Reality lies farther behind man: the sun rising is its traditional place, immutable center of his universe.

In a sense we also arrive here at the Odyssean crossroads. Gibson is dwarfed by the power of the sun just as surely as Hilton by his Saturnian vistas—man reaches his limits not only on the far extremities but at the familiar center as well. It is

at this point that Clarke affects his final, most radical redress-
ment: heavenly bodies again begin to move in tune to our
fundamentally human pattern, and in the boldest correspon-
dence yet Earth itself becomes son of the Sun. The ultimate
scene is a complex interplay of father-son relationships on all
levels. Gibson and Squeak walk outside the Martian dome to
watch the ship leave for Earth. In accordance with pulp conventions Gibson stays on to embrace his new life. And yet a part of
him returns as well—his spiritual "father" Hadfield has taken
his place. On another plane there is similar balance: the Martian "son" Squeak stands beside him on Mars as Jimmy goes
back. For an instant they look at him, he at them, and opposites
seem frozen in suspension: voyages out and back, real and
adoptive sons (Jimmy will marry Irene and thus become Hadfield's step-son—by other stranger laws Gibson has taken
charge of Squeak), planets lost and found (Gibson loses Earth,
Hadfield Mars, but only in each case to find a new home that
turns out to be an old one—Gibson watches a familiar sunrise
in the open "air"). Yet in spite of this the balance is tipped
subtly earthward. As Gibson watches the other Martian moon
Deimos he sees it suddenly become brighter. The new star
made by this earthbound ship not only balances but actually
overshadows the earlier incineration of the other moon—the
Mars-bound Phobos. That "Sun" will burn itself out. On
the contrary this new body (ship and moon) seems, as Gibson watches the fall to Earth, to be balanced by the true Sun
rising on a man-made Mars.

At first glance *Childhood's End* seems a very different
novel in theme and form—evolutionary pretense has become
transcendence, the individual adventure of boy or man a collective one of the human race itself. The germ of this broader
perspective already exists in *Sands*. There the Martians are
innocents; ostensibly, it is the contact with man that starts
them on their upward climb. More is at work here though than
evolutionary pressures. Science cannot explain why Squeak
(whose race otherwise lives in Rousseauist oblivion of men)
should suddenly follow Gibson and begin this renaissance.
Implicit in this "childhood's end" then (simultaneously a rise
and a fall, as Squeak learns malice from human civilization)
is the mystery of transcendence. In speculating about a "higher
being" as far above man as man above Martian, Clarke pre-
sents a series of races not so much linked by evolution as
separated by it: the only contact between such self-contained
compartments is transcendental. In *Childhood*, however, 49

this transcendent progress is nonetheless offset by the regressive rhythms of the old Odyssey pattern. Individual adventure does not disappear here; on the contrary, the novel is a series of such adventures—self-contained circles joined less by magical transitions than by ties of a basic human sort: those of family. If in each episode (though on different levels) the voyager-hero is a "son" rebelling against authority, in every one of them the discovery of manhood—whatever its state— invariably coincides with a reaffirmation of ancestral patterns: the going out is always a return to roots. In *Childhood* Clarke has shifted the Odyssean encounter—primarily between man and outer vistas in *Sands*—to the inner space of the family itself: Odysseus and Telemachus are telescoped, the alien immanent in the familiar patterns of formation and maturity, the most domestic of adventures. At this crossroads, the rise of a collective alien cannot be separated from that orphaned voice which, in mourning the demise of the free individual, gives poetic permanence to the family of man before the void.

In *Childhood* the familiar out-and-back rhythm continues to shape the narrative; its workings, however, have become much more subtle. What is more, this basic pattern has been transposed from the realm of space to that of time: progressive and regressive elements are incorporated in a larger interplay of sequency and simultaneity. Again there is a hint of this transposition in *Sands*, where the evolutionary journey of the Martians is offset by speculation that they once might have been a "higher race" themselves—evolving or degenerating, their path no longer runs only in a line, but in a circle as well. The new complexity of *Childhood*'s structure is immediately visible in the layout of its chapters, which are arranged in a progressively numbered sequences. But the chapters cut—in unbalanced fashion—across three larger sections that form the novel's core. If these sections differ from each other spatially (each has a different number of chapters), in a temporal sense they appear self-contained circles of more or less equal value, each framed by a prologue and epilogue in which the same situation is repeated, where time and space seem to interfuse in something like a *deja-vu* effect. In turn these sections are encompassed in a larger circle formed by the prologue and epilogue to the book itself. Yet in this chain of circles, again and again time is suspended only to resume its flow. But in which direction does it move, forward or backward? On one hand the static nature of the novel seems opposed by a real forward thrust: the prologue has a title, the epilogue does not. But if childhood's end is no end then, in what sense is this so? Man superseded in the end carries us back to a like suspension in the beginning: the two scientists immobilized by the coming of the Overlords. On the last page these same Overlords are leaving a spent Earth. And yet, paradoxically, though they move physically in an opposite direction, spiritually they are moving closer to man—they have become his proxy, the extension of his rebellious childhood, the new son of his Sun. The dynamics of *Childhood's End* resembles a complex gearwork, a mesh of circles that overlap and join in their opposite, counter balancing motions.

The structure of the first section, "Earth and the Overlords," is an example of this subtle interplay of progressive and regressive rhythms. Set against the forward movement of the story line are a series of mirror inversions. At the core we find a typical Clarkean opposition: Stormgren is kidnapped and taken to a cave deep in the earth where he confronts a mysterious Welshman whose "extraordinary eyes seemed to search his mind to the depths"; but if this seer turns out to be blind, Stormgren himself is no less blind when (in the corresponding episode aboard Overlord Karellen's ship in space) he futilely tries to shed light on the nature of the alien being. There is here—but in inverted fashion—a going forward after all, for the blind actually comes to see. Even if he sees a tail going out that door on the spaceship, thus equating Karellen with the devil (which is error), Stormgren nevertheless accepts him—on a new plane of moral vision the old breach between man and adversary is healed. At the same time, though, this going forward is a return. In the section's final scene Stormgren is neither below ground nor in space but rooted in his native woods: the rebellious son of man ("I was only sixty at the time") has become a patriarch. And in his final vision—Karellen coming to Earth to wander by the grave of the "first man ever to be his friend"—roles are even further reversed, for now the father of sin becomes himself the returning prodigal son. This twist touches off a series of similar reversals across the novel; but as the position of the Overlords is turned around, it is gradually deepened as well, rooted more and more firmly in human patterns until man's destroyers become his preservers. The fall of angels, we learn, is not myth but prediction: it lies not in the past but the future. And it turns out to be a most fortunate thing indeed. In the string of individual rebellions that comprise the novel—Stormgren, Jan—that of Karellen will be the last and most balanced: he will serve this time, 51 yet in that service will not lose his soul. The spirit of individual humanity is extended beyond its tomb. Indeed, if the end of *Childhood* is again a suspension of opposites—Last Man and Overmind—this time the third term and point of balance is the Overlord himself. He comes not to visit man's grave, but carries it with him in the form of Jan's lament. But balance here, as in the beginning, is again unstable. Perhaps Karellen's concourse with men has humanized him—he sees the Sun as a parent mourning its lost offspring Earth. Yet his final union with that Sun is more than poetic metaphor. The ending of *Childhood* seems to balance on an edge: on one hand there is cold logic—the Sun is just an indifferent source of power, a "dwindling" thing one turns one's back on; on the other there is empathy—Stormgren's lost son has, in his exile, become a grieving father too, for mankind. Characteristically, Karellen's final gesture is ambiguous, pointing two ways at once: "In silent farewell he saluted the men he had known,whether they had hindered or helped him in his purpose." In the novel Clarke will lavish all his art to tip the balance of this final hail and farewell unobtrusively, to bind Karellen even as he flies away, to ground him in Odyssean fashion in Earth and the family of man.

Each of these three central sections is framed by the same kind of episode—an "interview." Out of these pairs of confrontations the basic dialectic of the novel develops on parallel levels, themselves in constant contention: on one there is individual man's free will against cosmic plan; on the other there are sons against parents. More than antithetical or complementary, the true relationship between these two lines is contrapuntal. There is, however, in terms of the deeper meaning of this novel, a subtle slant to this dynamic. In the complex intermeshing of themes in *Childhood's End*, ahuman physical processes are constantly underscored by corresponding patterns that are eminently human. Thus men may pass indifferently to some other "higher" state of being, but in this persistent relation of father to son that permeates every corner of this novel man as traditional center continues to abide.

The first section begins with Stormgren's interview with Wainwright, head of the Freedom League, and ends with the nameless journalist coming to interview the retired statesman himself. In these paired scenes not only are roles reversed—a Biblical legend is neatly turned around as well. In the person of Wainwright it is ironically man, not the devil, who represents the position of *non serviam*—man must work out his own destiny. In the end, however, Stormgren has intuited (after his own abortive attempt to rebel) that those called "devils" may be on the contrary necessary and even beneficient guardians—man must not work out his destiny alone. The framing scenes of the second section again reverse this relationship of man to Overlord, only to explore its meaning more deeply. Again there are two interviews—Karellen reveals his being publicly, and calls a press conference to announce Jan's evasion. A triumphant entry then is set against a chiding exit—where one door opened for man two now slam shut ("the stars are not for man"). The erstwhile devil, who first in almost Christ-like fashion suffers the little children to come unto him, in the end must admit the loss of one of these children, and at the same time acknowledge (implicity) that for all his wisdom he may not have understood their needs. This revelation reaches back beyond this section to the first—the emphasis on the Overlord's mask-like face at this press conference reminds us of Wainwright's blind fanatical honesty, of the Welshman's mask. He who would be all-seeing is blind, and this "Golden Age" section reveals just how blind the Overlords have been in man's case. The world of Rupert Boyce's cocktail party is both frivolous and sterile—ironically these guardians have created a world in which there are no children. There is only Jan, the spiritual orphan, whose progress exactly reverses that of Karellen. Where the latter passes from initial harmony with Earth's children to his final lonely exit, Jan goes from the isolation of Boyce's rooftop to the discovery of a spiritual father in the scientist Sullivan at the bottom of the sea. Jan's trajectory is Stormgren's exactly, but on a different plane: a plunge to the depths takes him to the stars, only to bring him back to his native Earth again. What is more, on the Overlord planet, he discovers they too are bounded by the very same polarity—the Cyclopean Eye in the depths of their "museum," and the burning mountain of fire. But if man and Overlord are both held by the same limits—each are dwellers on the "flatland" between—in this revelation human gains mastery over his nominal lord. Ironically, it is these gods of reason who prove the more superstitious. At the bottom of Earth's sea Jan too discovered a blind monster; but the nickname man gave this beast—Lucifer—is one of affection, not fear. And if the planet Jan reaches is indeed hellish in aspect, this does not dampen his inquisitiveness but heighten it. The Overlords, on the other hand, who "draw the line" at probing the mystery of the great eye, irrationally "blind" Jan's camera eye as he seeks to photograph the magic mountain. In this new balance, the Overlords' superstitious reason pales against that human intuition that will ultimately burst these limits, linking with the "Overmind." There is in all this another, subliminal irony at work—these Overlords have become somehow more human than their charges: the ground has been laid for the final transfer of man's heritage from Jan to Karellen.

Indeed, in becoming Overmind, man will no longer be man. A final set of parallels, however, suspends even this ultimate journey—metamorphosis itself is balanced by the eternal return to human roots. The third section once again is framed by interviews: the Greggsons meet with a representative of New Athens; Karellen meets Jan, now the last man on an alien Earth. Between these two poles is set up a complex rhythm of comings and goings. In moving to the utopian colony the Greggsons seek to leave the world the Overlords made. This sterile cultural "revolt" is matched by one on a more fundamental biological level, one which moves in the opposite direction—spontaneously their own children begin to "unlearn," growing away from them. This anti-*bildung* in turn is matched by Jan's experience—a growing to maturity that coincides with reconciliaton, fleeing earth only to embrace it. Beyond this homecoming though there seems nothing but leaving: the "children" abandon Earth, Jan dies, Karellen sails away. At this point end and beginning join: final alienation recalls the parallel homecoming-in-estrangement of the prologue. Here, in the familiar world of our cold-war present, is another close encounter with cosmic mystery. Once again two beings insurmountably separated (they are on diametrically opposed sides, both politically and geographically) are united by a shared mystery. Clarke's two scientists are typical Odyssean heroes: representative yet exceptional men ("One Konrad Schneider was worth a million names on an electoral roll") whose adventurous probings are suddenly suspended in a passive moment of revelation ("He had labored to take man to the stars, and, in the moment of success, the stars—the aloof, indifferent stars—had come to him"). But this meeting with the alien, in another sense, is also a homecoming: as these "enemies" stand before the unknown they rediscover old bonds—their common German childhood, beyond that their common humanity. At the other end of the novel two adversaries of a different magnitude—Jan and Karellen—are also joined in separation. The advent of the Overmind hurls both back on past roots. But if Karellen mourns not man but "his own race forever barred from greatness by forces it could not overcome," this he discovers is little more than the mirror image of man's destiny as Jan represents it. As in the face of this alien web he now sees he has shared with man a common form after all, he realizes too that he shares his destiny. As opposed to that premonitory fall of angels, this turns out to be not a future but rather a past, and a human one as well—opposing the drive of Karellen's ship now is the pull of man's ancestral Sun, and not the Overmind.

If that Sun "dwindles" as Karellen moves away, in the texture of the novel itself it waxes stronger: as source and organizer of human life it gradually permeates the growing current of organic imagery in *Childhood*. The culminating balance is the unequal one of Jan and Overmind: new father and orphaned son. And yet it is on this unlikely plane that the inexorability of transcendence is first suspended, and this balance in turn subtly tipped in favor of dying mankind. The final section opposes two voyages: Jeff's "breakthrough," his mental journey to galaxies beyond the Overlord's comprehension; and Jan's adventure, narrated in Odyssean fashion at the point of return, ending in a homecoming stranger than any distant shore. The former prepares for transcendence, the latter leads to death. And yet, because each shares a common root, unbalanced opposition imperceptibly modulates into something else—a rhythm of flux and reflux, a cycle of life rather than radical change. For if Jan's role in the end is the epitome of individuality—the lyrical mourner of man's passing—this "breakthrough" too, though it leads to the alien, must "inexplicably" begin with a single human: the seed to which Jan returns is the one which begins this process—individual man. However undeniable or irreversible the fact of transcendence seems in *Childhood*, it is increasingly challenged on the level of poetic metaphor. Already in the Prologue the moment of change is subsumed in imagery drawn from the permanence of Earth's cycles: "This was the moment when. . . the present sheared asunder from the past as an iceberg splits from its frozen, parent cliffs, and goes sailing out to sea in lonely pride." All the way across the novel this echoing figure (with its strong pull backward) envelops and domesticates another alien breakaway—Karellen's lonely and prideful exodus. Throughout *Childhood* the unhuman processes of change are (on this poetic level) caught up in those natural rhythms most traditionally associated with human change-in-permanence: "It had been a Golden Age. But gold was also the color of sunset, of autumn: and only Karellen's ears could catch the first wailings of the winter storms." Over and over, at moments of rupture, "scientific" explanation is countered with this elegaic vision: Karellen's comparison of the metamorphosizing children to crystal formations is humanized by the mourning parents—out of this horde of dead faces George Greggson imagines Jeff turns to look back at him; on this level at least one of the book's masks comes momentarily alive. This same elegaic vision is carried to new dignity and power by the solitary Jan: as voice against the void, he rejects self-pitying "morbidity" (unlike Bradbury's Hathaway he refuses to light up man's dead towns) for the nobility of lament. In recording man's demise, his voice becomes a tribute to a form of human imagination the exact opposite of that which powered the "breakthrough." Instead of losing himself in the universe, he draws it to a point, seeing the stars "tangled in a ghostly spider's web." If as Jan claims the children's metamorphosis is not tragedy but fulfillment, a final neo-Homeric simile replaces this fulfillment at the heart of that organic life cycle whose culmination is not Overmind but man: "There was nothing left of Earth: *They* had leeched away the last atoms of its substance. It had nourished them, through the fierce moments of the inconceivable metamorphosis, as the food stored in a grain of wheat feeds the infant plant while it climbs toward the Sun." Science can turn away from ruined Earth, but poetry remains geocentric: if the new being is an advancement, it is also a regression, a parasitic vampire. The final pages of *Childhood* are Janus-faced: men become Overmind, ceasing to feel; Overlords learn to feel, and become men. We are left, in this evolutionary novel, with the old Romantic rift between mind and heart—as men we cannot help choose the latter.

Next to the intricate clockwork of *Childhood's End, 2001: A Space Odyssey* seems sparsely linear, a manifesto more than a novel, the transformation of the Odyssey pattern into self-conscious formula. Drawing strongly on that tradition of elegaic response leading back through Wells to 19th century English poetry, the structure of *Childhood* is itself eminently lyrical in nature: through delicate interplay of repetitive and contrastive patterns, a tension that is not drama but lyrical poignancy is gradually developed around the situations leading to that final encounter between Last Man and Overmind. In contrast *2001* seems dry, intellectualized, stylized. In this later novel the Odyssean adventure of modern scientific man is transposed from the lyrical plane to one which is primarily symbolic in nature. As a result *2001* tends to develop twice removed from the materials of the adventure drama it transforms—on a level that should perhaps be called "metaphysical." The lyrical response of the heroes of *Childhood* is still a human response. Here, cut away from even this grounding, Clarke's symbols seem to become murky as "philosophy" or religious statement, empty as human experience.

2001 is classic only in the sense that it is the epitome of Clarkean space adventure—a restatement of the out and back pattern which not only resumes all the stock devices of the early works but seeks to reconcile them with the transcendent ending of *Childhood*. In more ways than one the novel betrays its composite nature—a work made of earlier bits and pieces, put together after the fact to explain a film. It reads at times like a haphazard compendium of old themes and situations: there is the "Earthlight" epiphany—the familiar globe is suddenly alien, "a giant moon to the Moon"; there is the alienation of the spaceborn—the onlooker suspended "between hope and sadness" as Earth "like all mothers" bids farewell to her children. This in fact is primarily a novel of onlooking, of these maxim-like catch phrases which themselves epitomize the experience of excessively passive encounters. In long sections of *2001*, the voyager-man, as immobile as the moviegoer overwhelmed by the film's visual effects, confronts alien landscapes—Jupiter, Saturn, the Star Gate. Each confrontation is followed by its aphoristic resume: "The time had not yet come when Man could leave his mark upon the Solar System." Indeed, the influence of the film on this novel's structure is clear: Clarke's sententiousness is matched here by a new,almost facile cleverness very reminiscent of Kubrick's film version, where Clarkean formulas in turn are carried to a gratuituous degree of stylization. In skeletal form *2001* develops the same interplay of progressive and regressive elements as *Childhood*. Here again are a series of compartments—not only different adventures but different species as well—that are simultaneously self-contained and overlapping, evolving and not evolving. The classic example of Kubrick's treatment of these paradoxical transitions is the famous shift from Moon Watcher's Earth to Floyd's moon—the bone tossed in the air that becomes a spinning space station. If these are both weapons, then man (at least in his lethal capacity) has evolved. But he may also have regressed at the same time: the music changes from *Zarathustra* to a waltz. Both composers are Strausses, however. And which is "superior"—the mock 57 grandiose or the frivolous? It is this kind of intellectualized encounter—where emphasis is less on the man caught between home and eternity than on the mechanisms of entrapment and their meaning—that Clarke cultivates (though to a lesser degree of stylization) in *2001*.

This stylization can be seen in the working out of the complex web of father-son relationships at the heart of this odyssey. Things at first seem to evolve in the strictest linear manner. The slab instructs Moon-Watcher—this adopted son in turn becomes the father of mankind, bequeathing to it the same lesson of violence and war. His modern son Dr. Floyd has two sons in turn—Hal the thinking computer and Dave Bowman. If on their voyage out both grow up, Hal succumbs to guilt while Bowman, tempered in solitude, endures. The end of his voyage, however (as with the children of *Childhood*), is a regressive unlearning that leads paradoxically to higher being—Bowman becomes the Star Child. But once again transcendence coincides with the return to roots—the Star Child is also a homecoming Odysseus, the avenging bowman. The very neatness of this balance is mirrored in the schematic, almost didactic unfolding of the internal dynamics of the novel. Events read progressively can be read regressively as well: both Moon-Watcher and Hal—ape and machine—do not evolve so much as fall. It is hinted that Moon-Watcher's people once enjoyed an Edenic past—warm rains and lush fertility. Already fallen, the only movement can be forward to new destruction: the slab teaches him to kill for food; refining this knowledge, he teaches himself to kill for power. Hal's destiny is analogous: born of an "electronic Eden," this new Frankenstein monster is corrupted and led to kill by a split programmed into him— the disparity between truth and lie, ideal and real world. But likes, we discover, are also opposites. If Moon-Watcher advances from innocence to corruption, Hal as he is disconnected retraces this path to its source, reverting to that childhood from which Moon-Watcher escapes. These counter-movements create here an almost emblematic balance: on each side of man, ape and machine form a triangle—an epic age offset by a tragic one, extroversion by introspection. To survive Moon-Watcher is taught to sever his ties with the past. Hal, on the contrary, seeks to return to that innocent world by breaking all ties—he deflects the antenna aimed at an Earth that has become his "conscience." It is in fact this desire to be alone that leads to conflict with Bowman—the lyrical hero whose existence is neither adventure nor retreat but suspension between such opposites. Here at this static center the Star Child exists already. Bowman may travel to the limits of human possibility, but he discovers only the familiar: on the threshold of a new "order of creation" he finds the ancient order of the four elements ("Beyond the realms of sea and land and air. . . lay the realms of fire"). And his final impossible resting place turns out to be a banal Earth hotel room: "He was prepared. . . for any wonder. The only thing he had never expected was the utterly commonplace." Movement in either direction is resumed, in almost emblematic fashion, at this point. What was still temporal movement in *Childhood* is fixed here for ever, hieratically, in symbolic space.

The structure of *2001* then neatly suspends its representative hero between transcendence and return (Bowman balances the excesses of both Moon-Watcher and Hal by living his existence in reverse at the moment of apotheosis), but in doing so bypasses the elegaic encounter altogether. Where such exist in the novel, they are transposed to a symbolic level—emphasis shifts from human brushes with cosmic mystery to external phenomena which themselves come to stand for such encounters. There are no meetings with Mercurians; instead a bullet probe is fired at an asteroid, or the spaceship bounces "like a ball on a cosmic pool table" off Jupiter's gravitational field. Out of this futile disproportion comes a flash of balance: "Against the darkened portion of the asteroid there was a sudden, dazzling explosion of light." With man out of the picture, the shift from micro-to macrocosm becomes imperceptible: on the other side of the Star Gate the giant red Sun bears the same relationship to the pinpoint "White Dwarf" that orbits it. Yet on both sides of this gate (and on whatever scale) the relation of smaller body to its "parent" is always one of violence. The Dwarf draws a searing column of flame across the Sun by the mere fact of its gravity. The Star Child returning to Earth does much the same as he explodes the orbiting nuclear weapons: are we to assume the same blind physical necessity behind his act? In *2001* man appears caught up in a play of cosmic forces; the balance achieved is one beyond good and evil, indifferent to human will or desire. The Star Child's statement that he is "master of the world" is echoed verbatim by Moon-Watcher—yet neither is his own master. And if (as his name predisposes) Watcher's violence is aimed out at the stars, that of Star Child (in accordance with this inexorable balance) will be necessarily directed back to an Earthly source. Star Child's detonation of the bomb is paralleled by

59

Moon-Watcher's killing of One-Ear: both acts are neutral rather than moral, petulant children playing with new "toys." At the focal point of this chiasmus of power we find not man but slab. In itself the obelisk seems to enfold the Odyssean opposition: a mathematical series extending endlessly into new dimensions, yet ever grounded in a point, the already perfect symmetry of the object itself. Whatever the slab is, it raises a question: if the universe imposes its rhythms on man, to what degree does man impose his on the universe? The very blankness seems to tip the balance back to man; this time, however, the Odyssean roots may be blighted. Both going out and coming home in the world of *2001* are paths of violence and corruption: Moon-Watcher claws his way upward only to end in Bowman's hotel-haven where home has become a sloppily-built illusion; Star Child in turn goes back to an Earth so polluted that the only "cleaning" possible is destruction. Has the encounter with the alien become here, at the same time, an encounter with our own fallen selves—not so much suspended as trapped between ape and god? This doubt echoes through Clarke's latest two novels, where a clearly skeptical view of man's capacities in the face of cosmic mystery inflects the Odyssey pattern, mitigating both adventure and homecoming. In these novels lyrical dignity gives way to satire, elegiac nobility to something closer to foolish impotence.

The theme of *Rendezvous with Rama* is itself the compartmentalization of man: the novel not only depicts his helplessness before the mysteries of the universe, but seeks to deflect some of the blame for that helplessness back on man as well. The analytical, satirical thrust of this "rendezvous" is betrayed not only by the frivolous overtones of the designation itself but by the microscopic nature of the situation—the space odyssey structure of *2001* is literally turned inside out here, the mysteries of outer space bounded in this floating nutshell. Once again the inspiration for *Rama* is a composite one: the idea of a ship tapping energy from a sun is posited in *Childhood*, the possibility of an interstellar voyage in hibernation raised in *2001*. In *Rama*, however, Clarke has shaped these old themes to new satirical purposes.

The Odyssey pattern is not superseded here. On the contrary, it is made to function so that its bases can be examined: if there is for man a simultaneous voyage and homecoming, what is the nature of these eternal roots to which he returns? The satirical shift is already visible in *2001*, in the portrait of Floyd and the moon scientists before the slab: the lyrical encounter has become the source of wry jest at human vanity and folly; man has become the stupid tourist before the mysteries of the universe. The world of *Rama* is filled with such deflating moments. In its texture this is a book of empty discussions and wranglings, futile heroics, where the exhiliration of space walks has become the tasteless observation of female breasts in weightlessness. Icarian adventure is now performed by "aerobatic" cyclist Jimmy Pak. Indeed, each of his crewmates is haunted by some frivolous pastime or popularized past: Commaner Norton lives in the shadow of Captain Cook; the violation of the Raman building is carried out by Joe Calvert, a fan of old bank-robbing movies. Always at the verge of mystery the pull is back to the trivial: before the strange Raman artifacts Norton feels like a "monkey" reaching for "the reflection of a banana in a mirror." The ending of the novel, in fact, is a piece of tongue-in-cheek transcendence. The revelation that Ramans do everything in threes may simply mean that two more ships are on the way. But it may be a "breakthrough" as well, a moment of human contact with the alien. The same thought occurs, in totally unrelated contexts, simultaneously to both Norton and Dr. Perrera—the former in space yearning for home, the latter comfortably dreaming in bed. More significantly, however, this union is not double but triple: Norton is with Laura. But they are not lovers—the form of man and woman is present but there is no substance. Nor can the union of any of these people lead to something meaningful: here is a triad more sterile and unyielding than Rama's own triple silence.

Imperial Earth, Clarke's latest novel, is a huge elaboration of this same reductive dynamic. As Clarke's most deeply pessimistic view of man's capacity before the infinite, of his evolutionary and transcendental inviability, it stands as a corrective to the elegaic humanism of *Childhood's End*. The voyage here exactly reverses that of the earlier novel—the hero goes back to Earth only to reveal human roots as shallow as space is deep. At a Pascalian middle between empty point and void of space, the accent falls less on man's lament than on his helplessness and its causes. For it seems, in *Earth*, that man is physically menaced on both extremes—by "Star Beasts" from without, and from within by the "fingers" of the asymptotic point drawing matter to its "death." Yet it is clear that man himself has created these menaces: his new drive has caused a "flaw" in space; the Star Beasts may be "corpses. . . of executed criminals." The source of flaws 61 in this novel is man himself; throughout the book Clarke probes the blighted root with satirical fingers.

If in one sense *Earth* is an anti-*Childhood's End*, in another it marks a return to textural density (too dense in fact to be dealt with adequately in the space remaining). The leisurely pace of the new novel may lead the reader to think Clarke has taken a step beyond philosophical parable or lyrical novel here, toward real men, their socioeconomic preoccupations, their lives and loves. This is not so. Economics and intrigue have served Clarke before (in the early *Earthlight* as well as the late *Rama*) as raw material to be worked into Odyssean correspondences and suspensions. If anything, Clarke's view of man in *Earth* is the opposite of sympathetic or tragic. Insofar as it functions on a human level at all, it is a scrupulous anatomy of man's labyrinthine attempts to escape from the physical and moral boundaries that hold him, and which may ultimately be of his own creation.

For this, a near-utopian setting seems perfect. But if most things are possible in 2276, the old patterns strangely recur: this new Earth, like Britain of old, has become "imperial"; in seeking the new, man finds himself enslaved to ancestral forms. The symbol of this finiteness in infinitude is the polyominoes: though the frame is changed at will, the pieces retain the same shape. And so it is with the pieces of this future puzzle on Earth: on Titan we find a "Loch Hellbrew," on Earth an "Island of Dr. Mohammed." In this novel where nothing moves in linear fashion, the alien is telescoped on the familiar, all players caught in a rhythm of expansion and contraction. Calindy holds Karl's soul in her hand like an egg; but this egg (a "tactoid") turns out to be an object of protean possibility. In like manner, Karl breaks this bondage to envision the Argus antenna that no human eye can span. Duncan and Karl meet for the last time at the blind center of Cyclops: here too constriction radiates outward—this time to impossible reunion; Duncan will clone Karl, not himself, choosing the future, not the past. And yet Karl's vision, reborn of the "minisec" which holds life in its hands, will instantly shrink to a point—the tiny sea-urchin Duncan has randomly killed. If this rhythm regulates man, he tries to regulate it as well. The attempt to focus matter at the "node" of the A-drive causes it to expand in other, destructive directions—this tiny point could wreck Duncan's entire economy. In this framework the transcendent encounter becomes highly ambiguous. The overlapping of large and small, Argus and sea-urchin—

the same unusual shape "in two quite independent contexts"—leads to Duncan's revelation. But is this immanence or coincidence, significant or empty form? And out of this new hole Duncan wills posterity—Karl's single cloned cell—what will emerge, new being or old?

If the transcendent moment has any locus in *Earth*, however, it is in the family. On this level the novel clearly reads like a parody of *Childhood's End*. All the principal figures act out traditional relationships, yet there is no real blood bond between them. Grandma Ellen and Armand Helmer, Karl's father, are cousins. But Ellen is only nominally "grandmother" to clone Duncan—he and the blond Karl then, if they are Dioscuri, are false ones. And is not Catherine Linden Ellerman, by some strange kind of osmotic contraction, the daughter that the fated union of Grandma Ellen Killner and Captain Kleinman never had? The new child at the end of the novel will be the fruit of another empty love—this time the triple union of Duncan, Karl, and Calindy. The family world of *Earth* is both incestuous and sterile: it is out of this web that the transcendent seems to emerge, reversing the general genetic "reversal" of the novel, creating life out of a dead past. But does it? Karl's clone will not carry the defective Makenzie gene; and yet Karl in his earlier incarnation did not reproduce—his sterility is of the mind, romantic love, and Duncan would resurrect him for just this "theoretical" vision. If in the polyomino pattern Karl's clone is that cross of rare Titanite, this beauty proves only another vertiginous center, a plunge into the void. Karl's homecoming may well be such: "The little head was still empty even of dreams. . . But already the smooth, pink scalp bore that unmistakable trace of hair—the golden hair that would soon bring back to Titan the lost glories of the distant Sun." The recipe is present here, not only for future triumph, but for Icarian fall. What is more, that Icarian past is a singularly banal one—his fall was a "brain burning" with a "joy machine." Nor is the look forward more reassuring—there lie the hollow voices of space. As dynasty has become a curse (the Makenzie's missing letter), so the Odyssey pattern itself, instead of suspending man between cosmic beauty and vital past, has become a prison. The polyomino configuration that links Duncan and Karl has only two permutations, and one is merely the reverse of the other. Karl substituted for Duncan then is no transfiguration, only a reorientation of the same "flaw." In *Earth* the Odyssean roots—alive still in the elegiac poetry of *Childhood's*

End—are blasted. Man is contained in new limits no longer physically neutral or even traditionally humanist. Behind Clarke's growing satirical vision lies more than a hint of theology—the primal curse.

BIOGRAPHY

ARTHUR CHARLES CLARKE was born December 16, 1917, at Minehead, England, the son of Charles Wright Clarke (a farmer) and Nora Willis. He attended King's College, University of London, and received his B.Sc. there in 1948. After years of working as an auditor for the British government, and later as an editor for *Science Abstracts*, he became a full-time freelancer in 1951. He lives and works in Colombo, Sri Lanka (formerly Ceylon). Among his best-known works are *Against the Fall of Night* (1953), later revised as *The City and the Stars* (1956); *Childhood's End* (1953); *Earthlight* (1955); *2001: A Space Odyssey* (1968); *Rendezvous with Rama* (1973), and *Imperial Earth* (1975). A collection of memoirs and reminiscences, *The View from Serendip*, was published in 1977.